A deadly enemy se

When an old jo

hands, he and Bo

caught up in a search for a lost excavation site and the secret it hides. But the journal holds more than meets the eye.

Already at odds with dangerous local rivals, Maddock and Bones soon find themselves in another race with a clandestine organization called the Trident, who are bent on securing a lethal prize.

Can Maddock and Bones survive what lies deep within the CAVERN?

Praise for David Wood

"A page-turning yarn blending high action, Biblical speculation, ancient secrets, and nasty creatures. Indiana Jones better watch his back!" *Jeremy Robinson, author of SecondWorld*

"With the thoroughly enjoyable way Mr. Wood has mixed speculative history with our modern day pursuit of truth, he has created a story that thrills and makes one think beyond the boundaries of mere fiction and enter the world of 'why not'?" *David Lynn Golemon, Author of Ancients*

"Let there be no confusion: David Wood is the next Clive Cussler. Once you start reading, you won't be able to stop until the last mystery plays out in the final line." *Edward G. Talbot, author of 2012: The Fifth World*

"I like my thrillers with lots of explosions, global locations and a mystery where I learn something new. Wood delivers! Recommended as a fast paced, kick ass read." *J.F. Penn, author of Desecration*

"Dourado is a brisk read, reminiscent of early Cussler adventures, and perfect for an afternoon at the beach or a cross-country flight. You'll definitely want more of Maddock." *Sean Ellis- Author of Into the Black*

CAVERN

A DANE MADDOCK ADVENTURE

DAVID WOOD
TERRY W. ERVIN II

CAVERN
Copyright 2018 by David Wood
All rights reserved

Published by Adrenaline Press
www.adrenaline.press

Adrenaline Press is an imprint of Gryphonwood Press
www.gryphonwoodpress.com

This is a work of fiction. All characters are products of
the authors' imaginations or are used fictitiously.

ISBN-13: 978-1-940095-95-0
ISBN-10: 1-940095-95-6

BOOKS and SERIES by DAVID WOOD

The Dane Maddock Adventures
Dourado
Cibola
Quest
Icefall
Buccaneer
Atlantis
Ark
Xibalba
Loch
Solomon Key

Dane and Bones Origins
Freedom
Hell Ship
Splashdown
Dead Ice
Liberty
Electra
Amber
Justice
Treasure of the Dead

Adventures from the Dane Maddock Universe
Destination-Rio
Destination-Luxor
Berserk
The Tomb
Devil's Face
Outpost

Arcanum
Magus
Brainwash
Herald
Maug
Cavern

Jade Ihara Adventures (with Sean Ellis)
Oracle
Changeling
Exile

Bones Bonebrake Adventures
Primitive
The Book of Bones
Skin and Bones
Venom

Jake Crowley Adventures (with Alan Baxter)
Blood Codex
Anubis Key

Brock Stone Adventures
Arena of Souls
Track of the Beast (forthcoming)

Myrmidon Files (with Sean Ellis)
Destiny
Mystic

Sam Aston Investigations (with Alan Baxter)
Primordial
Overlord

BOOKS and SERIES by TERRY W. ERVIN II

Thunder Wells

Monsters, Maces and Magic
Outpost
Betrayal
Guild

Crax War Chronicles
Relic Tech
Relic Hunted

First Civilization's Legacy
Flank Hawk
Blood Sword
Soul Forge

Dane Maddock Universe
Cavern

Collections
Genre Shotgun

Prologue

"Do you believe she has any idea where we are going?" Baufra kept his voice low, scarcely above a whisper. The High Lady Qalhata had remarkable hearing and she never seemed to miss a trick.

Harwa flashed him a warning glance, his eyes wide with alarm.

"Are you mad? We never question a High One. Never!"

Baufra nodded. He didn't trust the High Ones. They were an odd lot, and he wasn't just thinking of their physical appearance. Everything about them was just a little bit… off. Their limbs were too long, their torsos too thin, their eyes too large. Even their pattern of speech, the way they worked their lips with each syllable, as if human speech were unfamiliar to them. Some said they were gods, but Baufra knew better. Three days ago, the High Lord Intef had fallen, his heart pierced by an arrow from one of the primitives that called this land home.

An arrogant man, Intef had ordered everyone to stay back as he alone approached the natives. He'd spoken in a tongue utterly alien to Baufra and the others. Either the natives had not understood either, or they'd grown bored of what he had to say, because in the middle of Intef's speech, one of them had raised his bow and fired a single shot that found its mark.

Baufra still remembered it all. The blank expression on the primitive warrior's face as he took aim, the sound of the arrowhead piercing flesh, the look of disbelief in Intef's eyes as he turned back toward his men, the casual disinterest with which the natives watched him die. And then the battle.

Baufra and his men had driven the natives away, slain several. But not before they had stolen Intef's bow and arrows. Some of his men had wanted to try and track down the thieves—the bow was a priceless treasure—but the High Lady had ordered them to continue their journey, insisting that their destination was somewhere close by.

Three days later, they were still wandering.

Baufra hated this land. It was cold and damp and smelled of earth. And the natives were a constant source of danger. They had no metals, their weapons were of wood and stone, but they had the advantage in numbers, and they moved like shadows through the forest. Half of Baufra's party had lost their lives on this journey. He wondered if any of them would make it home.

"Baufra!" The High Lady Qalhata called in that strange, birdlike trill she called a voice.

Baufra knew not to delay. He hurried in the direction of her voice until he found her, standing in a tiny clearing, gazing down at that strange silver tablet she always carried.

Baufra dropped to one knee in front of her and lowering his gaze. "You called, High Lady?"

"You may rise."

Baufra stood, eyes still downcast. He hated looking at the High Ones.

"I have found it," she said simply.

Baufra's head snapped up and he met her gaze. Hope flickered inside him. Perhaps this journey was almost over.

"You are certain?" He forgot to add the honorific, but Baufra didn't seem to care.

"It is underneath us. We need to find a way in."

"If I may ask, High Lady, what are we looking for?"

"A cavern. That is all you need to know. Now, find the way in. That is all." She made a shooing motion with one long-fingered hand.

Baufra bowed and hurried away. The sooner he and his men could find this cavern, the sooner this nightmare would be over.

It was nearing nightfall when Baufra and Harwa returned. They had successfully completed their task, and found the cavern. But what they discovered within its depths gravely concerned him.

"Should we tell her we found it?" Harwa asked.

"I don't see how we can avoid it," Baufra said. "It's not far away or well-hidden. Sooner or later it will be discovered."

"You saw what's down there. We could be here for years before the task is completed."

Baufra forced a grin. "Then we had best get started as soon as we can."

When they reached the camp, Baufra knew immediately that something had gone very wrong. There were too few men here; only a handful milled about, all looking fearful. The closest man, a soldier named Irgo, spotted the newcomers and hurried over.

"The natives. They attacked us again in even greater numbers."

Baufra gritted his teeth, anger burned inside of him. He should have been there to fight, but deep in the cavern, he'd been blissfully unaware of what transpired above.

"How many lost?" Baufra asked through gritted teeth.

"All but four."

"And the high lady?"

Irgo shook his head slowly. "Gravely injured. I fear she will not survive the night."

A burst of relief flooded through Baufra. If the High Lady should pass, that would leave him the highest-ranking survivor. He would order the party to return home immediately. Surviving the return journey would be a challenge, but that was a problem for another day. Perhaps he ought to feel guilty for taking pleasure in the death of another, but the High Lady had never shown even a passing concern for the many losses they had suffered on this journey.

"She wanted to see you the moment you returned," Irgo said.

"Very well. Set a perimeter around her pavilion. Everyone keeps watch for now. I'll not lose another man to these savages."

While Harwa and Irgo went about setting up defenses, Baufra went to see the High Lady. A single oil lamp sat on the ground beside her pallet, giving off faint golden light and a musky perfume scent.

Qalhata lay on a pallet on the soft earth. A blood-soaked bandage was wrapped tightly around her middle.

Baufra winced. No one survived a wound like that.

"My Lady," he said, dropping to one knee beside her.

Qalhata opened her eyes and gazed blankly at the roof of the pavilion. "Did you find the cavern?"

"We did, My Lady." Baufra described what he and Harwa had found deep in the cavern. As he spoke, Qalhata smiled.

"Take me there," she whispered.

"My Lady, I fear that is impossible. There are places where we must crawl, or climb great distances. In your condition we would have to drag you along. You would not survive it."

"I will not survive if I simply lie here and wait for death. But if you can take me there, I would have a chance."

Baufra tensed. He had suspected that the cavern was a source of great power. By the gods, he had felt it! Was it possible? Could the High Lady be healed? And even if it were possible, was that what he wanted?

His left hand slipped to his dagger. No! It would be too obvious. He would have to suffocate her. His hands twitched and then he came to his senses. He had killed many times but he was not a murderer. He was a man of honor.

"It will be as you say, High Lady."

"You will take me, along with the man called Irgo. He will know what must be done with my body should I not survive. In this, you will follow his instructions. Do you understand?"

"I do." Baufra's head spun. Irgo, the low-ranking soldier, knew of the High Ones' crafts? What else did he not know about his traveling companions?

"You will lay me to rest in a place worthy of one of my standing." She coughed and winced. "And there is one other thing. As you know, I must be protected in the next life."

"I am certain every one of our men would be honored to serve you." Baufra highly doubted that, but it would be done.

"I require the noblest of our number. That means

Irgo and yourself."

Baufra listened with a powerful sense of detachment. Maybe he should have been shocked at the knowledge that he might die very soon, but for some reason, it didn't surprise him. Of course his fate would be sealed just as he stood on the cusp of freedom.

"Very well, High Lady. But we shall make every effort to assure that you do not reach the next life any time soon." He bowed his way out of the pavilion and hurried to find Irgo. He might never leave this land, but perhaps he could avoid leaving the world any time soon.

1

Connie dipped her paddle into the water, careful not to clack the blade against the gunwale of the canoe. She'd already done it once, eliciting a sharp rebuke from Nelli. Connie loved her sister, but sometimes Nelli could be a downright pain. Pushing the thought aside, she focused on the task at hand—paddling silently through the dark waters of the Little Miami River. Out here on the water, beneath the night sky, with only the whisper of the wind through the reeds and the occasional cricket's chirp or croak of a frog to break the silence, it was easy to forget that they weren't all that far from Cincinnati.

"Paddle on the right," Nelli whispered. "I want to get out of the middle of the river."

"Why? Are you afraid the Frogman might spot us?"

"That's exactly what I'm afraid of," Nelli hissed. "Well, afraid isn't the right word. I just don't want to scare him away."

"Right," Connie mumbled. "Because he really exists."

"I heard that."

Connie rolled her eyes and kept paddling. Why did she let Nelli talk her into these crazy things? When they were kids, Nelli had been fascinated with unsolved mysteries. At age twelve, she'd canvassed their neighborhood in search of witnesses to an abduction that had taken place ten years earlier. Of course, she'd brought Connie along as a pack mule to carry her notebooks and oversized tape recorder. They managed to hit about ten houses before someone called their mother. As the years went by, Nelli's interests expanded to include lost treasures, the supernatural, and cryptids—creatures like Bigfoot and the Loch Ness Monster. Thanks to her sister's domineering personality, Connie now had a misdemeanor on her record for trespassing in an alleged haunted house, although the charge was soon to be expunged from her record, provided she stayed out of trouble.

"Are you sure we're not going to get busted?" she asked.

"By whom? And for what?" It's not illegal to take a canoe out on the river.

Connie sighed. Nelli was probably right. And even when she wasn't right, she wouldn't be dissuaded.

"I still can't believe you actually think giant frog people live in the river."

"They aren't giant, at least not compared to a human," Nelli said. "They're only four feet tall, maybe five."

Connie gritted her teeth, wondering if a joke about their comparative heights was coming. Connie was of average height, but Nelli stood 5'10" without heels or hairspray, and she never let Connie forget it. But the joke didn't come.

"And I don't necessarily believe that the Frogman exists; I just think it's worth investigating."

Connie rolled her eyes. "Because of one crappy photo a drunk teenager took with his cell phone?"

"Yes, and I don't care what anyone says. That photo can't be easily explained away."

I don't care what anyone says. That summed up Nelli in a nutshell. She was older, more forceful, even taller than Connie, and she sometimes lorded it over her. Connie bit back a retort. It was her own fault for letting

Nellie push her around. Which was the reason they were now out here searching for a four-foot tall frog-human hybrid with big glowing eyes.

"Connie! Look over there!" Nelli's soft whisper scarcely reached her ears.

"You can't scare me, Nelli."

"I'm not joking. Look over there to the left. Just beyond that fallen log."

Connie scanned the shoreline, wondering what had caught her sister's attention. Probably a boulder or a stump. Every shadow seemed to be alive on a night like this.

And then she saw it. A dark, hunched shape moving near the shoreline, a faint, unearthly glow surrounding it.

"Keep the canoe still. I want to get pictures."

Connie's heart raced. Cold sweat dripped down the back of her neck.

"I'd rather just turn around and go back."

"Not a chance."

The camera's shutter click sounded like gunfire in the silence. Another click, then another. Connie's heart thrummed a rapid beat. Could that thing, whatever it was, hear the sound of the camera? What would it do if they drew its attention? She tried to tell herself there must be a rational explanation for what they were seeing, but she couldn't quite make herself believe it.

"I need to get closer," Nelli whispered.

"Hell, no!"

"I can't get a good angle."

"I do not care," Connie said slowly, emphasizing each syllable. "I am not getting closer to the shore."

Nelli let out an exasperated huff of breath. "Fine.

Maybe if I stand up I can see over those reeds."

Before Connie could protest, the canoe wobbled.

"Nelli, don't stand up in the canoe."

No sooner had the words passed her lips than the canoe lurched to the side. Connie let out a curse as the two young women plunged into the frigid water. Connie went in headfirst. The river was deeper than usual, thanks to heavy rain. In an instant she found herself fully submerged. Her clothing quickly became waterlogged and her shoes filled with water. Suddenly held down by their weight, she felt fear course through her and she began thrashing about. Her hand struck something sharp, a lance of pain shooting up her arm. She opened her eyes to the freezing water, which stung her eyes as she searched the darkness for any sign of the faint moonlight that would guide her to the surface, but all was black.

Something grabbed her foot and she opened her mouth to scream. Water poured in, choking her. Panic threatened to overwhelm her as she yanked her foot away from the clutches of whatever held her. The Frogman?

And then her foot came free. Through the haze of fear, she realized nothing had been holding on to her except the soft sand of the river bottom. Now free and properly oriented, she swam for the surface. The current and her heavy clothing fought against her, and she struggled to suppress the urge to cough, brought on by the water she'd inadvertently sucked into her lungs. She kicked and paddled but remained underwater.

Why didn't I wear a life jacket? I'm a grown ass adult and I know better.

Her lungs burned, a sensation like ever tightening

iron bands circled her chest and throat, and she saw spots before her eyes.

It can't possibly be this deep? Am I going to die?

And then her head broke the surface and she sucked in a ragged, wet breath of sweet air. She began to cough and sucked in another mouthful of water. She fought to keep her head above water, but it was a losing battle.

Where is the canoe? If I can grab hold of it I can keep afloat.

Something collided with her.

"Connie?" It was Nelli! Before she could reply, Nelli grabbed her by the hair. "Help me! I can't stay afloat."

Connie closed her eyes as she was forced under the surface again. She had read about this—a drowning person became so panicked that she would take others down with her in her struggle to remain afloat. She fought to break Nelli's grip on her, but her sister was out of control. No sooner had Connie managed to untangle Nelli's hands from her hair than Nelli began kicking like Chuck Norris after too much espresso. A sharp, bony knee caught Connie in the forehead, followed by a kick to the gut that forced the air from her lungs.

Dizzy, out of breath, and exhausted, she stopped fighting.

That's it. I give up.

She sank, frightened but beyond caring.

And then powerful arms circled her chest and hauled her upward. She was dreaming, hallucinating. Or maybe an angel was carrying her up to heaven?

She broke the surface again, reflexively took a deep breath. Her throat burned and her body was like lead.

"Just lie back," a voice said in her ear. "Keep breathing, float if you can, and let me take you to shore."

She tried to ask about Nelli, but all she could manage was to keep sucking in life-giving oxygen.

After what felt like an eternity, her heels struck the riverbed and their progress halted.

"Here, let me help you stand," the voice said.

She found her footing and, with support, managed to stand on wobbly legs like a newborn foal. In the faint light, she could finally see her rescuer. He as a sturdily built man of above average height, short, blond hair, and light colored eyes. Maybe blue?

"Don't worry," the man said. "Your friend is okay. My buddy's got her."

Relief flooded through her, turning her knees to rubber.

"Easy," the man said. "Do you need me to carry you?"

Connie shook her head slowly. "No," she gasped. "I'll be all right." The man helped her make her way to the shore where she plopped down on the soft earth. To her right, she saw Nelli being helped to shore by a huge man with long, dark hair. The moonlight highlighted his facial features, revealing him to be Native American.

"Who are you?" Connie asked.

"That's Bones." Her rescuer pointed at the big man. "And I'm Dane Maddock."

2

Maddock and Bones took a moment to make sure the two women were all right. Both were soaked and had breathed in too much water, but each was quickly getting her breath back and recovering her wits. In Maddock's estimation, they had to be sisters. The same auburn hair, straight nose, and wide, engaging smiles as they laughed at something Bones said. No points for taste, Maddock thought.

The taller woman was at least five-ten. Her hair was cropped short, and she appeared to be in her mid-twenties, thin but curvy. The younger woman, Maddock guessed in her early twenties, was a few inches shorter and had her hair pulled back in a ponytail. She lacked her older sister's attributes, having a more athletic build instead.

"So, you want to tell us who you are and what you were doing out on the water this time of night without life jackets?"

"I'm Danielle," the older woman replied, shaking Bones' hand. "My friends call me Nelli. This is my sister, Constance. Connie for short."

Maddock offered his hand. Connie was slow to shake, her green eyes making only brief contact with his. Her hands were slightly calloused, with short, unpainted fingernails.

"As for the life jackets, we were stupid."

Bones nodded. "Well, we got you out of the water and your canoe ran aground a little way down the river, so no harm, no foul."

"Except for my camera." Nelli held up her camera. Water dribbled out from inside it. "Ruined."

"You're a photographer?" Maddock asked.

Nelli ignored him. "Why were the two of you creeping around late at night?"

"Creeping around?" Bones turned an incredulous look at Maddock. "You're lucky we were out here at all."

Nelli scowled at her ruined camera.

"Thank you," Connie said, "on behalf of me and my ungrateful sister."

"Sorry," Nelli said. "I'm just embarrassed and angry. Please don't think I'm not appreciative. We probably wouldn't have made it to shore without your help."

"What were you photographing?" Maddock kept his tone light, conversational, even though he could tell the young woman was hiding something.

A tense silence hung in the air, finally broken by Connie's tired sigh.

"We were looking for the Loveland Frogman. We saw something moving along the shoreline. Must have been one of you guys."

Maddock scratched his head. "The what?"

"The Loveland Frogmen," Bones chimed in. "It's a cryptid. More like, *they* are cryptids. There's more than one."

Maddock managed a tight smile. Of course Bones knew all about it. His friend loved legendary creatures. He'd been fascinated with them long before their days in the SEALs, and their adventures since then had only served to stoke his passion for the legendary and mythical.

"Big frogs that walk on two legs," Bones explained.

"They were first spotted back in the 1950s."

"How would a frog walk on two legs?" Maddock asked.

"They're not literal frogs," Bones said. "At least, probably not. More likely they just bear some resemblance to frogs. Leathery skin, webbed hands and feet. They might even be…"

"Don't say aliens."

"…aliens," Bones finished. "A small group crash landed somewhere around here and have managed to survive."

"Or somebody went to see *The Creature from the Black Lagoon* and got a little spooked on his way home," Maddock said.

"There have been some reliable witnesses," Nelli said, emboldened by her unexpected ally. "A police officer got a good look at one and gave a thorough description."

"And recanted later," Connie said.

"Years later, after he and his family had endured too much ridicule. And he didn't recant. He just says it was some sort of large reptile."

Connie rolled her eyes and then turned a pleading glance in Maddock's direction. Maddock shrugged. It seemed unlikely, but he and Bones had seen too many crazy things to dismiss legends outright.

"So what brings you out here?" Bones asked. "This isn't Loveland."

"There was a recent sighting in this area. The witness even took a photo," Nelli said. "A squat, grayish looking thing with huge, glowing eyes, coming up out of the water. We wanted to check it out."

Connie locked eyes with Maddock, jerked a thumb

in her sister's direction, and mouthed *She wanted to.* Maddock chuckled.

"We've told you our story," Nelli said. "Your turn."

"We were doing a little metal detecting," Bones said.

"Here? In the middle of the night?" Connie appeared unconvinced.

"We didn't want to be seen," Maddock said.

"What were you looking for?" the younger sister pressed.

"Pirate treasure," Bones said. "Nicholas LePetomaine's hoard, to be exact."

Nelli's eye went wide. "Fat Nicholas? Nasty Nick? His treasure is supposed to be buried in Eden Park."

"You really know your stuff," Bones said, clearly happy to have found a kindred spirit. "We were running down a clue in an old journal. No luck. We were getting ready to pack it in when we saw you capsize."

Nelli stood and sized Bones up. Although she was tall, he still towered over her. "So, you guys are treasure hunters?"

"Among other things," Bones said.

"In that case." She smiled and bit her lower lip, the effect marred by her bedraggled state. "I just came across the legend of a lost treasure not too far from here, and I don't think it's one many people have heard of, if any. We're free tomorrow if you two would like to join us."

Bones and Maddock exchanged glances. The pirate treasure appeared to be a dead end. Might as well take up a different hunt. He nodded.

"We're in."

3

The narrow highway wound through rolling green hills. The sign up ahead read, "Hocking Hills State Park." Bones breathed a sigh of relief, shifted uncomfortably, and turned to the Maddock.

"Did you show the rental car lady your junk, Maddock?"

Dane Maddock shot a confused glance at his friend. "What are you talking about?"

"I figured you must have, because she gave you a tiny car to match."

Maddock smirked. "It's not my fault you're too abnormally large for normal modes of transportation."

Bones chuckled. "The ladies like my abnormal largeness."

"Never mind, Bones." Maddock turned up the radio, Bruce Springsteen's rough voice drowning out the big Cherokee's wisecracks.

Bones reached over and turned down the radio.

"Enough with the white people music," he said.

"I thought you only considered country music to be 'white people' music," Maddock said, keeping his eyes trained on the road.

"Springsteen skirts the edge. He's like middle-aged folk emo. Really, how many songs about unemployment and shut-down factories can a guy write?"

"Heresy," Maddock said. "Tell me about this park we're going to. Did you learn anything about this supposed treasure?"

Bones grinned. "You suck at changing the subject, you know that? Anyway, no, nothing about the treasure. Nelli was right. It's not common knowledge."

"Or, it might total crap."

"You do this every time, you know?" Bones asked. How did Maddock manage to hold on to his skepticism after all they'd seen?

"Someone has to be the voice of reason."

"Until he's proved wrong." Bones held up a hand and began counting on his fingers. "Atlanis, Loch Ness, Noah's Ark…"

"All right. I get it. Maybe there's something there, and maybe a woman who doesn't even have the good sense to wear a life jacket is the only one who knows about it."

"Dude, what is it like to be you? Can you even take a crap with that tight sphincter of yours?"

"I knew you had an interest in men's sphincters," Maddock said.

"Screw you, Maddock. I mean, not that. Oh, forget it," he said over the sound of Maddock's laughter. "Anyway, the park sounds like it's worth visiting even if there's no treasure. Cool hiking trails, rock formations, waterfalls. And two babes meeting us there."

Maddock nodded. "Better than sitting around with you watching *Ancient Aliens.* No Bigfoot sightings in the area?"

"As a matter of fact, I did find a website that mentions Bigfoot."

"I vote we focus on the treasure. Did Nelli give you any background information?" After the rescue, Bones and Nelli had spent a lot of time in quiet conversation, leaving Maddock to try and find common interests with her younger sister, a college student.

"She said there were two brothers that lived in some of the caves there, back in the late eighteenth century. They stole a treasure from the local tribe. Might have been gold, or sacred relics, no one seems to be sure. She called it the Two Brothers Treasure. Said she found the account in an old journal written by a local man. He wasn't famous, so the journal hasn't really been studied. It's just part of the collection of their local library."

Maddock gave a thoughtful nod.

Bones continued. "Anyway, the natives finally tracked them here, well into Hocking County. They caught them and tortured them, but the brothers never told where they hid it. Supposed to be buried somewhere in the park. No one's ever found it." Bones grinned. "According to her, no one's even looking for it."

Maddock shrugged. "That's really not much to go on. Is there more?"

"A little bit," Bones said. "The way the legend goes, a hermit lived in the area and searched half his life for the treasure. He believed if he stood in the right spot at midnight, he'd hear the ghosts of the brothers whisper where the treasure is hidden."

"Has anyone actually heard it?"

Bones shrugged. "Park closes at sunset, so nobody, except maybe park rangers, would ever have a chance to hear the ghosts."

"Maybe we should have gone at night." Maddock was skeptical of the veracity of most ghost stories, but recent events had convinced him that not every ghost story was false. "I'm guessing you did some independent research?"

"A little bit. Couldn't sleep. Here's what I've got. Pat

and Nathanial Rayan lived in the park area, maybe the main cave around 1795. They might be buried in or near the cave, nothing definitive I've found yet. That's the only account I could find of brothers being connected with the park."

Maddock quirked an eyebrow. "Did you find anything about either of them being killed by Native Americans?"

"We aren't like white dudes when dealing with thieves. We hide the evidence."

Maddock shook his head and smiled before he and Bones discussed what places in the park might be of interest.

Maddock pulled to a stop at a T intersection. Brown signs with white lettering indicated the way to turn to reach the state park's various attractions.

Maddock looked west, through the windshield. He didn't need a forecast to tell rain was on the way, but not immediately. "Do we want to hit Old Man's Cave first?" The other two they'd decided upon as potentially the most interesting were Conkle's Hollow and Rock House.

"Unless the girls have another plan, maybe hit Conkle's Hollow last," Bones said. "Sounds like it's named after some white dude's—"

"Conkle's Hollow it is," Maddock said, interrupting his friend's crude joke. While they'd brought rain gear, from what Bones described, Old Man's Cave and Rock House probably had more natural shelter formations.

A short while later they pulled off State Route 374 onto a side road. A minute later they rolled into a small parking lot tucked between a picnic area that included several tables and a relatively new and modern restroom facility on one side, and a recently sown field on the other.

Nelli and Connie were standing near a stone wall next to an old cast-iron hand pump. The sun was low in the sky, behind the cover of clouds. It was a little on the cool side for a spring morning, with an occasional gusty breeze to emphasize the point.

"Glad you could make it," Nelli said. "I tried to call and let you know where to meet us, but no joy." She pulled her cell phone from her back pocket. "No signal out here. Happens every time."

Bones checked his cell. "Yep. Lost our signals just after we turned off Route 33."

Neither woman showed an ill-effects from the previous night's adventure. They were alert and appeared ready to go. Even Connie was all smiles.

The four set off together. As they made their way toward a wooden bridge that led across a wide stream, Maddock tried to keep the conversation going.

"So, you know the park and surrounding area pretty well?"

"I visit here a lot, like my sister said." Connie pointed to the tall flowers among the scattered sapling maple and oak trees. "If we were here on a sunny afternoon," she said, casting a baleful glance at the gray sky, "we'd see Eastern Swallowtail butterflies and Hummingbird Clearwings, and maybe some Ruby-throated Hummingbirds."

It was Maddock's turn to nod. "Too bad about the weather, then."

Connie shrugged and lapsed into silence.

They walked along a boardwalk spanning a marshy area before coming to the beginning of the Conkle's

Hollow trail and followed it down to a sign reading Rim Trail. Tall trees, many having grown straight up without branching out, striving to reach sunshine ahead of the others, filled the area. Beneath them, ferns and other ground plants covered the brown leaves that remained from the previous fall. The second set of steps and trail cut into the rock formation, winding up the hillside. If they went up one set, the trail would lead around the gorge and they'd return down the other.

Nelli untucked her shirt from her jeans and tied the ends in a knot, putting her tight stomach, and emphasizing her ample bosom. Bones clearly took notice, and Nelli pretended not to be aware of his attention.

"Which way?" Bones asked.

"I prefer the Gorge Trail," Connie said, sensing her sister's concern. "More scenic." The last time they took the rim trail, her sister complained about the climb. She wouldn't want to look bad in front of the two men accompanying them.

Bones tapped his boot on the sidewalk. "Urban scenic?"

Nelli took Bones' arm. "It isn't paved the entire way."

"It'll help keep you from getting lost," Maddock chided, "like in that corn maze last fall."

"Screw you, Maddock. Corn mazes are for rednecks."

"We can always take the Rim Trail afterward," Connie said. "Or move on to one of the other sites."

Maddock had to admit, the trees, flowers and ferns, the skittering lizards and tiny fish in the shallow stream that meandered to their left, between the trail and the moss and vine-covered Black Hand sandstone cliff of the hollow, it was refreshing. Not as isolated, lush and filled with wildlife as the Amazon, but possibly in the top ten the Midwest had to offer.

A little farther down the trail the group stopped to look up at a bulging, bark-covered growth on a tree, like an encompassing knot larger than its trunk.

Maddock pointed out various aspects of the growth, then concluded, "Looks like a snapping turtle."

Connie disagreed. "More like a Ninja turtle."

"You guys are blind," Bones said. "Pac-Man."

Nelli was about to give her opinion when a voice sounded from somewhere down the trail, further into the hollow. The trees, plants and two-hundred-foot cliff walls both captured and muffled the distant words, but not so much that they couldn't be made out.

"Go to hell, old man." The deep voice carried menace. "It's none of your damn business, so get moving." A few seconds later it continued. "Am I gonna have to bitch slap your old, scrawny ass?"

For a fraction of a second Maddock and Bones exchanged glances before they moved side-by-side down the path. "Stay here," Maddock said to their companions.

Maddock and Bones raced ahead, not at a full sprint, both watching and listening as they came around a small bend. They spotted an old couple easily in their late sixties moving their direction, the old man shuffling while looking back over his shoulder.

"Come on, Harold," the old woman scolded in a hushed voice, tugging her husband by his hand. "We can find a ranger and let him deal with them."

The couple stopped as Maddock and Bones approached. Maddock slowed and asked, "Are you all right? What happened?" Bones went around the couple, not breaking stride.

The woman started to say something, but the old man cut her off. "Three dirtbags are vandalizing the rocks back there." He pointed with his thin walking stick.

Maddock nodded. "We'll take care of it." He ran to catch up to Bones, who was approaching the group.

"Hey, assclown, get back on the trail."

"Did he say 'assclown'?" Nelli had ignored Maddock's instructions and followed them. Connie was not far behind.

"It's his favorite word. Along with asshat."

A heavily-muscled young man glared at Bones. "You talking to me?" Maddock recognized the voice as the one that had threatened the old elderly man. He wore a white sleeveless shirt sporting a Confederate flag on the front. A muscle-bound weightlifter, Maddock assessed, probably assisted by steroids, judging from the blond-haired man's rampant acne. He was at least as tall as Bones.

The two other men with the loud-mouth thug were both between five-ten and six foot, and appeared to frequent the gym as well. They wore jeans and boots and T-shirts advertising fast cars and firearms. Unlike their bigger friend, who'd had his hair cut to mere stubble, they sported unruly mops hanging below their ears. Maddock was surprised none of them wore a battered John Deere cap.

It was apparent one of the three had been trying to scratch something into a boulder that had fallen away from the cliff decades ago. It looked like the beginnings of an arrow.

Bones folded his arms. "You answered to the name

assclown, so yeah, I must have been talking to you."

The young man cocked his head in disbelief before he began striding down from the defaced boulder, back toward the cement trail.

Without looking at them, Maddock said, "Stay back. We'll handle this."

"That's Derek, a local," Connie said. "Wrestled for some Big Ten school on a scholarship a few years ago. Flunked out. I think he works as a bouncer in Columbus, but he's been telling anyone who'll listen he has a tryout with the WWE next week."

"He looks big and mean enough," Nelli whispered back.

Derek made his way down the hill, grumbling, "What's with all these damn Indians lately? They don't sell cheap liquor in the park, so I don't what's here that they might be interested in." Swaggering more as he got closer to Bones, Derek flexed his thickly muscled arms and clenched his fists. "What kind of man wears his hair in a ponytail?"

"Your mom didn't mind it last night," Bones said. "You should grow one, too. I'll bet your boyfriends would love it." Bones nodded in the direction of Derek's companions.

"I'm gonna rip that thing off your head and stick it where the sun don't shine." Derek gritted his teeth and his pimple-riddled face reddened.

"So you're pulling hair and talking about men's butts?" Bones took a serious tone. "Look, kid, you don't want to do this…"

Derek charged.

Bones stepped in, caught the larger man around the waist, and performed a judo-style hip toss. Derek landed flat on his back among a patch of ferns.

Maddock moved to interpose himself between Bones and the other two troublemakers as his friend looked down Derek.

"Give it up, dude," Bones said. "It's not going to end well for you."

One of Derek's companion's charged at Bones. Moving quickly, Maddock kicked the attacker's legs out from beneath him. The young man hit the ground hard but quickly clambered up on hands and knees. Maddock drove a knee into his temple, sending him slumping back to the ground.

Maddock took no pleasure in taking down men who were a good ten years his junior, but they were thugs who needed to learn an important lesson: There's always someone out there tougher than you.

With a threatening finger, Maddock pointed at Derek's other friend, who wisely lifted his hands in a placating move and took a few steps back.

Derek, however, was a slow learner. He got to his feet and turned, rubbing the back of his head.

"You're about to do something stupid, aren't you?" Bones said.

Again, Derek charged, just like before. Same move.

This time Bones had a half second more to prepare. Stepping back he delivered a right uppercut to Derek's chin. The blow staggered the musclebound bully, but he kept coming. A left cross ended the contest.

Bones shook his left hand. "Damn, that dude's jawbone is dense."

As if to emphasize the point, dazed, Derek struggled to push himself to his knees, blood dripping from his mouth. He gritted his teeth, tensed himself to spring, and then collapsed to the ground again.

Derek's companions hauled him to his feet. The duo didn't argue as Maddock demanded their IDs. Using his phone, which he confirmed had no bars, he snapped a quick photo of each, vowing to report them to the authorities if the three did anything other than leave the park immediately.

"Or we'll track you down and deal with you ourselves," Bones added. The big Cherokee grabbed the men's wallets from Maddock and took all the cash from each.

"You're stealing from us?" Derek grumbled.

"You three vandals are making a donation to the park, since you just defaced it." Bones looked at the older couple Derek had harassed earlier. They stood with the two girls, nodding in approval. "Will you two put this in the donation box at the trailhead?" They nodded in unison, accepted the cash, and hurried away.

"Do we need to follow you three to make sure you don't give anyone a hard time?" Bones asked, handing them back their wallets.

Each assured them that they would be no further trouble. Maddock and company watched them until they limped out of sight.

"Well," Nelli said, reaching out and taking Bones by the hand, "you guys sure know how to show a girl a good time."

4

As they followed the well-worn trail, Connie enjoyed pointing out various caterpillars, mosses and mushrooms to Maddock, while Nelli asked Bones about the places he'd visited.

Eventually, the four reached the trail's end. After taking some selfies and a timed snapshot photo with Nelli's cell phone, Bones and Nelli explored the waterfall streaming down from a fissure between the rocks, splashing onto a flat boulder, while Maddock looked back the direction from which they'd arrived. Connie moved to stand next to him.

"If you look at it from just the right angle," Maddock said, "everything looks pristine."

"Most people like the waterfall better," she said, "but I agree with you. This view is one of the best, even better when the sun is shining down."

Maddock crossed his arms, looking up at the gloomy sky. "You know a lot about this park, and the surrounding area?"

Connie stared down into the shallow, grit and pebble-filled stream flowing from the falls. "Some. More than most visitors. Less than a lot of the locals."

"But you never heard anything about a treasure?"

She looked up at Maddock, one eye squinted. "Not until Nelli found that journal entry. What's your deal, anyway? Are you two as crazy as my sister?"

"Just a couple retired Navy SEALs, always looking for a little adventure."

She smirked. "That's why you two took down Derek and his friends so easily. For a second, I was kind of worried for your safety."

Maddock laughed.

"So," Connie said, "are you and Bones rich from your all treasure hunts?"

"No. Sorry to disappoint you, we're not rich. Interesting to be around, sometimes, but not rich." His face turned serious. "There are more important things in life than money."

It was her turn to laugh. "I already figured that one out, or I wouldn't be studying Natural Resources." She pointed with her thumb over her shoulder. "Nelli, I'm not so sure. Heck, when she finds out Bones doesn't spend his nights rolling around on a pile of doubloons, she might not find him so interesting."

Bones glanced over his shoulder at Maddock and Connie, having caught some of the conversation. He looked like he was about to say something, but Maddock caught his eye and waved him off.

"So," Maddock asked Connie, "where would you recommend we visit next?"

Without hesitation, she said, "Rock House."

"Awesome," Bones interjected. "If it's anything like the Hard Rock Café, I'm all over it."

The trail leading down to Rock House was a narrow dirt path. Erosion and the roots of the maple trees that lined the path made the way perilous. Chipmunks skittered about and a few birds flew from tree to tree.

"The trail going out is better," Connie said to Maddock. "And Rock House itself is pretty neat, right

Nelli?"

A few yards ahead of them, Nelli was too engrossed in another of Bones' tales, this one about him and Maddock scuba diving in some of Oak Island's water-filled shafts and tunnels, to even hear a word her sister said.

"Keep an eye on my sister," Connie whispered. "Before we climb up into the cave, it's likely that for some reason unbeknownst to her, one or more of her shirt's buttons will mysteriously become unbuttoned."

Maddock chuckled. "That won't bother Bones one bit."

"I had a feeling."

After climbing a set of carved stone stairs and making a short hike along a rim trail, the four reached Rock House. The layered sandstone was a faded yellow, mixed with grays and reds, many places covered by a thin layer of green moss. Climbing up and through one of the wide fissures in the Black Hand sandstone wall was easy enough. Nevertheless Bones helped boost Nelli up one of the high steps in. Maddock offered to help Connie. She just rolled her eyes and waved him off.

The cave inside had a high ceiling, about twenty five feet, hidden in shadowed darkness. East and west ends of the cave, spanning almost seventy yards between, each had a large opening that led to steep drops. There were several smaller openings along the north wall, which faced out above the rim trail. Since the cave was only about ten yards deep, the openings provided ample light, even on the cloudy day.

Rock House's floor was damp and worn, with a few shallow puddles. Three couples and a family with three young children explored the cave's small alcoves and climbed around on the worn rock ledges.

Maddock gazed out through the openings. What he saw was picturesque, especially to the west, where the drop off was both immediate and extensive. In places, small plants, vines and moss added their green to the cliff face that rose far above and below the cave. Entire oak trees that had fallen lay against the wall at the bottom, extending up only a fraction of the cliff's height. Birds flitted among the leaves and crevices.

Maddock listened to rustling above, tucked somewhere in the ceiling and pointed out to Connie where the sound was coming from. All the people talking and the resulting echoes made the effort mildly challenging. The few areas of bird droppings confirmed his assessment.

"Bats?" she asked.

"Birds. See, a pigeon," he added when one of the birds roosting dropped into the light, flapping its wings, and flew from the cave.

A little boy wearing a harness and strap shouted, "Bird, Mommy. Look!" He shot away from his mother, pointing up and chasing after the bird.

The mom, who was tying her daughter's shoes, looked up and shouted, "Billy, Stop!"

Billy didn't listen. She grabbed for the strap but was a fraction of a second too slow. He raced after the bird, looking up, unaware of the danger ahead of him.

Both Maddock and Bones saw what was about to happen—the boy running right off the cliff.

"Holy crap," Bones said, even as he sprang into action. Both he and Maddock were sprinting toward the west end of the cave.

The mother screamed, "Stop, Billy—Billy!"

There was no way they were going to make it. Maddock was a half stride ahead of Bones. He dove, right hand outstretched in an effort to reach the trailing strap.

The boy kept running, looking up, but he slowed to look back at his mom just before tumbling over the edge. Maddock's fingers were three inches short of the strap when it flicked away, following the young boy over the ledge.

Horror-filled screams, like those from a crowd watching a suspenseful slasher film, echoed throughout the cave.

Bones made it to the edge and peered down. Maddock got to his feet and looked over his shoulder. Connie restrained the mother who was fighting to go after her son.

"I see him," Bones said. "His harness caught. He's okay."

"Everyone stay back," Maddock ordered. "Connie, Nelli, keep everyone back, while I climb down and get him."

By the time he turned, Bones was already lowering himself over the edge.

Just then, it started to rain. Not a torrent, but well beyond a sprinkle.

"You couldn't wait for a port-a-potty, could you, Maddock?" Bones called.

"Just concentrate on what you're doing," Maddock called.

He looked over the edge, spotting the boy and immediately seeing the path Bones had to take. The little boy had only fallen fifteen feet. His harness strap had caught between a small crack in the sandstone and a small shrub of a tree that was growing out of it. It was another seventy feet to the rock and boulder strewn bottom, a fall that the boy wouldn't survive. Neither would Bones. His friend was an expert climber, but a free climb was always a risk.

The boy, initially battered and shocked, was becoming aware of his peril and began to cry.

Cords of muscle stood out on Bones' shoulders and arms, showing the strain of the climb, as his feet sought what little purchase there was so that his hands could move lower, allowing him to descend until he could reach the boy.

"Maddock," Bones said, his voice strained as he moved his left hand to a purchase eight inches below where it had been. "Tell those freaking tourists to do something useful."

Maddock shot a glance over his shoulder. Nelli was talking to the mother trying to reassure her. Some of the observers were crying.

"Like what, Bones?"

"Tell them to sing 'Rain, Rain Go Away,' or something."

Maddock almost laughed. "Right, Bones. You come back up here and lead the chorus, and I'll go down."

"Hey there, little dude," Bone said, dismissing Maddock's offer. "Don't move. I'm coming to get you."

How the Velcro and plastic clips of the boy's harness had managed to hold, Maddock didn't know. How long they would hold the dangling child was even less apparent.

Behind Maddock, the crowd had grown, as evidenced by the hushed murmurs. He heard Connie demanding that everyone give up their shoelaces. Nelli sounded like a company CEO as she once again ordered everyone to stay back. Give them room to work. The echo within Rock House only added to the effect.

Bones was about two-thirds of the way down to the boy when he suddenly exclaimed, "Holy crap."

"What is it?"

"Tell you later, Maddock."

The little boy started to cry louder and tried to grab ahold of the wall, causing him to slowly spin.

"Kid, I'm almost there, but I need you to watch me. Keep an eye on me." Bones slid his right-hand's finger tips into a vertical crack and lowered his left boot from its precarious perch, seeking another. Despite the sandstone's porosity, wind was beginning to whip the rain, making his descent more and more difficult. "Tell me if I'm doing something wrong, because I want to get to you faster."

To Maddock's amazement the little boy looked up, despite the rain striking is face and silently watched Bones descend to his level. Finger tips holding him in place, almost like a spider clinging to a wall, Bones assessed the situation. The boy had stopped spinning, but the wind was causing him to swing five or six inches, back and forth. How was he going to get the kid back up?

The boy's harness rig was oversized, the buckles and Velcro pulled to their tightest setting. The fact that it was made for a five year-old instead of a two year-old was what saved him, for the moment. How long the strap would remain caught, the plastic clip holding it to the harness, and the Velcro and clips holding the kid within the harness, was anyone's guess.

Bones figured the kid wasn't strong enough to hold onto him. Nor could he be relied upon to remain calm. He knew there was little chance he could climb with only one hand, especially now that the cliff face had become slick with rain. He'd have to attach the kid to him with his harness somehow, maybe through his belt?

The next thing Bones knew, Maddock was lowering a rope to him, one ending with a belt attached so that it could be looped around the boy and tightened. Where had Maddock gotten a rope? Then he noticed, it wasn't a real rope, rather a cord of...shoe and boot strings, twisted and knotted together.

Dubious as it looked, it was the only solution at hand. "Maddock, you didn't cheat to earn your knot-tying merit badge, did you?"

"Connie gets the credit," Maddock replied. "She says she'll send down a hangman's noose next, if you don't get it in gear."

"Might be preferable to riding back in that dinky car with you, Maddock."

The boy was shivering now, starting to whimper and kick.

"Hold still, kid." While Bones spoke he slid the belt up along the boy's legs and cinched it tight under his arms, and used the slack Maddock gave him to loop and secure the boy against what he expected to be a rough ride up.

The fingers in Bones' left hand were beginning to cramp. He knew that soon his calf and shoulder muscles would begin to burn, making the task more difficult. Despite this, he kept his voice steady. "We got this, kid."

Bones heard and saw the harness's Velcro straps begin to give.

Seemingly oblivious to his peril, the boy asked, "Did you see the bird?"

This kid was a cool customer, Bones thought. Or he freaking loved birds.

"Sure did. Now, grab your belt with both hands, and hang on."

The rig was janky as hell, but all that was available. He glanced at the belt one more time. It was a woven flexible one and should hold even if the kid let go. The rest of the rig gave him an added measure of insurance, the best available.

"Uh huh," Billy said, scrunching his face, holding his breath and hanging on to his belt as if for dear life—which he was.

"Go to it, Maddock," Bones said, holding on and keeping out of the way as best he could.

Bones watched, hoping the harness strap would lift out of its snag as Maddock and a heavily bearded African American man worked to gently lift the boy.

As soon as the kid was safe and over the side, cheers erupted.

"They better give me twice that," Bones muttered, the greater measure of his strength already spent. He had enough strength and skill, but the rain and wind wasn't helping. And no way was that dinky rope going to be of any help.

Bones exhaled and prepared to begin his ascent when Maddock said, "Heads up, Bones."

A multi-colored rope made up of a dozen or more shirts dangled next to him in the gusting wind.

"I suppose it's too much to hope that a bunch of Hooters girls donated these," Bones said.

A rousing round of cheers and applause met Bones

after he clambered back into Rock House. To his disappointment, only men had donated their shirts to the cause. And half of them were old, wrinkled white dudes.

Someone with a local carrier had managed to get a cell signal and contact the ranger station. After Maddock and Bones assured themselves that Billy was okay, and declined several requests to pose for cell phone photos, they made their way out of Rock House.

The trail down was narrower, often requiring single file hiking. The trail and steps were more challenging for the ladies to navigate, with Maddock and Bones often offering them a hand as they wound their way back up toward the parking area.

"You thought pretty quick on your feet," Maddock said to Connie.

She grinned and turned away, blushing. "You guys did the dangerous stuff."

Nelli took Bones' arm as the trail widened. "You took the biggest risk." She smiled up at him. As her sister had predicted, a few buttons on her shirt had magically come undone.

"He's the most expendable," Maddock joked.

"Screw you, Maddock. Besides, your white-dude eyes would've missed what I saw."

The rain had slowed to a drizzle as they made their way across the parking lot. A few people sat in their vehicles, waiting for the rain to subside, while others sat in the shelter house area.

"And what would that be?" Maddock asked.

Bones looked around, conspiratorially. "Tell you in the car."

5

"I saw something weird when I was climbing down," Bones said as they drove to their next stop.

"Was it your reflection?"

"Screw you, Maddock," Bones said as the girls laughed.

"It was a reasonable question." Maddock forced his grin into an expression of interest. "Okay, what was it?"

"There was something carved deep in the stone." Bones used his hands to show as he explained. "In a recess, angled away from the trail below."

Connie's and Nelli's eyes widened, but Maddock, sitting behind Nelli in the driver seat, merely nodded.

"A petroglyph of an archer," Bones added.

"Petroglyph?" Nelli asked.

"A prehistoric stone carving," Connie answered. She quickly added, "There's a visiting professor at my college. I attended two of his lectures. Most recently he's done some archeological studies around the Serpent Mounds. He's Native American," she said, but then frowned. "I don't remember what tribe—or group, if that matters. Sorry."

Bones shrugged.

Maddock asked, "You said it was weird, Bones. How so?"

"It looks old, Maddock. But not old enough for Native Americans to have carved it." He rubbed his chin in thought. "None of the local tribes that I'm aware of are known for their petroglyphs."

Maddock shrugged. "Graffiti isn't exactly a new

phenomenon. People travelling west have added their own carvings to historical sites."

Bones shook his head and muttered, "White people." He paused. "But then again, you can't exactly stumble upon that particular spot. You'd have to climb down there on purpose, and believe me, it wasn't an easy climb."

Maddock nodded. "Strange."

To accommodate large numbers of visitors, the main parking area near the Old Man's Cave trail was divided into three levels dug into a hillside. Narrow areas of green space containing scattered pine trees framed steps going down from level to level, until they reached a road running between the lots and the Visitor Center.

The Center was a brown, single-story building housing restroom facilities, a small nature exhibit, and a little snack shop that offered ice cream and the equivalent of fair food—hot dogs, nacho chips, soft drinks, bottled water and candy.

Nelli pulled her Jeep Wrangler into a spot nearest the Visitor Center. Back at Conkle's Hollow they'd decided to all ride together in her Jeep. Maddock counted only six vehicles, including theirs. She clicked off the windshield wipers. "The rain appears to have driven just about everyone away."

Nelli snapped closed her rain jacket and flipped its hood up to protect her head. "No sense waiting for what may never stop. Let's do this."

"This way," Connie said, pointing to a set of steps leading down to a small bridge spanning a stream that dropped into a waterfall. The steps carved into the rocks, supplemented by concrete reinforcement, made the trek down easy.

They came to a pair of signs. One pointed left. On it was written: Upper Falls. The other pointed right. On it was written: Old Man's Cave.

Bones strode forward and examined the sign pointing right. He announced, "I think I'll steal this sign."

"What for?" Maddock asked.

"To put on the front door of your condo."

That drew laughs from both Nelli and Connie.

"If I remember," Nelli said, "Upper Falls will take us past the Devil's Bathtub."

"Sounds like a great place to skinny dip," Bones said.

Connie rolled her eyes. "Not unless you want to drown."

"Upper Falls first, it is," Maddock said. "The rangers will get a kick out of rescuing a buck naked Cherokee."

It wasn't far down the Upper Falls Trail before the four came to a stone bridge reaching across Salt Creek, whose current had been boosted by the morning's rain.

Connie pointed down to a swift fall off in the creek where the water swirled into a roughly twelve-foot diameter drop before draining out and continuing northeast. It looked like a wide stone funnel draining foamy brown water. "That," she announced, "is the Devil's Bathtub."

"Looks more like a giant flushing toilet," Bones observed.

"After a dry summer," Connie said, "water sometimes just trickles in, more like a pool."

"I take it back," Bones said. "Nobody wants to skinny dip in a toilet, flushing or not. That would be like getting a giant swirlie."

They hiked their way along, Connie leading through the rain as they straddled puddles and climbed heavily worn steps carved into the stone decades ago. Maddock observed that the park's main attractions were too well travelled to have much chance of harboring anything secret or hidden. Still, something was biting at his senses, like he was missing something.

They reached the Upper Falls. A stone bridge spanned above the falls as the water cascaded down, forming a wide pool which drained off along the right, enabling Salt Creek to flow toward the Devil's Bathtub. To the right and left of the falls were deep crevices and alcoves that could only be reached by wading or swimming across the pool, or climbing down from above. Maddock suspected thousands had done both over the years.

Along the shore to the right a young couple stood, both soaked to the bone but enjoying each other's company too much to care.

"Now here's a place to take a dip," Bones said.

"Maybe if it weren't cool and raining," Nelli replied. "Except for you and Maddock, it would've been a dreary day. Connie and I would've given up and found something else to do."

Connie led the group up another set of stone stairs, and around to the bridge overlooking the falls. As she and her sister observed the water racing over the rocks toward the falls, Bones scanned back across the gorge.

Maddock noticed the look on his friend's face.

"Someone's following us," Bones said quietly.

Maddock realized that's what he was sensing but couldn't place a finger on. They hadn't seen anyone on the trail. The steady rain was keeping visitors away. "Could be those punks from Conkle's Hollow."

"Whoever it is, they're keeping their distance."

They both watched and listened as the ladies took photos of the rushing water with their cell phones.

"We'll keep our eyes and ears open," Bones said.

Maddock nodded once in agreement. Why did trouble always seem to find them?

6

The trail that led to Old Man's Cave was picturesque. Bones enjoyed the view from within the gully. The layers and curves of glaciers, and then water, had cut over the centuries, carving into the stone...the moss and ferns and trees, some with gripping roots exposed as they sprouted and grew among the walls, clefts and overhangs...he took it all in. He examined the rock formations, such as the protrusion of rock extending from the rim above the gorge, almost like a thick surfboard, or a giant's tongue.

That, he thought, might be one of the places where, at night, a ghost could be heard. Of course, if one ghost was talking to another, it didn't look like a formation where two would stand and converse. Maybe one atop would speak to one below? He shook his head, thinking it might be too far from the cave itself.

Ghosts were interesting enough, but they weren't his biggest interest, not compared to various cryptids. He'd have to do more reading up on them, ghosts and hauntings in the future. He'd seen plenty of paranormal, ghost-hunting shows. Maybe a few of those? Anyway, these would be ghosts of old white men. Trying to narrow the place where their voices might be heard, he'd have to think like them. He should start looking for the most idiotic locations possible.

Maybe he should ask Nelli? She was kind of hot, and they shared many of the same interests. Any girl who loved cryptids was a girl Bones could get on board with.

Maybe Derek and his friends…the humorous notion brought to mind the lingering, itching sense of being followed. He stopped and listened. Sensing something was amiss, even Nelli stopped talking.

Maddock apparently recognized the look on Bones' face. He listened and scanned the rim above the gorge, then shook his head. Nothing. Obviously thinking about the treasure legend, Maddock asked, "You hearing voices?"

Bones shook his head again. "All this rain's left water in my ears."

Connie frowned. She scanned the overhanging canopy. Although the sky had temporarily cleared, wind above the gorge had begun whipping through the trees, rattling their leaf-filled branches. The walls of the gorge protected them from that, but probably wouldn't protect them from the deluge that was on the way. "Looks like a storm's coming."

This time Maddock and Connie took the lead, picking up the pace. They made it through the tunnel and halfway across the arcing stone bridge that would deliver them at the foot of Old Man's Cave when the sheets of water began cascading down.

With rain hoods up, all except for Bones who only had his leather jacket, they raced up the steps into the large cave cut into the sandstone stone. It reminded Bones more of an oblong amphitheater than a cave, reaching about fifty yards deep its deepest point. But colloquial names tended to stick.

"Wow," Nelli said. "Barely beat that one."

After a boom of nearby thunder, Connie said, "We seem to be the only ones foolish enough to be out wandering the trails. At least we weren't walking a rim trail."

Nelli pulled back her rain jacket's hood. "I think we should stay here a while."

Connie began making her way across the cave, over to a stone pedestal with a metal plate on it. Nelli followed. Pointing to it, the younger sister said over her shoulder, "That tells the history of this cave, and I think it mentions the hermit who lived here."

Maddock and Bones followed them over.

Nelli read the history, running a finger over the raised bronze lettering. "It names the hermit, Richard Rowe, but it doesn't say anything about a treasure."

"If there was one," Connie said to her sister, "do you think the Park Service would write about it here?"

Nelli blushed. "Probably not."

"Well," Bones said with a smirk, "as long as we're stuck here, why not look for any unmentioned hidden treasure? It's sort of what me and Maddock do."

Connie and Nelli walked the short distance to the north end of the cave and began searching together, discussing what to look for. With a more experienced eye, Maddock began at the south end, his eyes methodically following from top to bottom the sediment layers and formations, looking for something out of place. Bones moved to where the floor met the cave's wall and did the same.

Within a few minutes, Nelli shouted, "Hey, Bones, come look at this!" Even though seemingly muffled by the downpour, her voice echoed off the walls.

Connie was running her fingers along a groove about six feet above the cave floor, right at the cave's edge. She managed to avoid a narrow rivulet of rainwater streaming down, forming an overflowing puddle that drained over the ledge, down the sandstone cliff and into the creek below. Just as Bones arrived, and before Maddock was halfway there, Connie jumped back as a section of rock the size of a football dislodged and splashed into the puddle.

"What'd you find?" Nelli asked.

"Water coming down eroded the sandstone, around that rock." Connie pushed the oblong stone with her boot, which looked more like gray limestone than the more common reddish sandstone. "My finger and rain coming down must've broke it loose."

"Look!" Nelli said while reaching into the revealed cavity, the same time Bones and Maddock said, "Wait!"

She withdrew her hand, holding what looked like a brittle leather pouch. "What?" she said, almost dropping it.

"On archeological digs, they're meticulous and take photographs and notes," Connie explained.

"Oh well, this isn't a dig."

Maddock said to Nelli, "Your sister's right. We really should have left it *in situ* and notified someone."

"Might be nothing," Bones said. "Is there anything inside the pouch?"

"Hold your hands out, Sis," Nelli said and gently used her finger and thumb to open the pouch before dumping its contents into Connie's cupped hands.

Triangular, glossy blue stones gleamed there, their worked edges glistening under the beam of Maddock's Maglite.

"Turquoise arrowheads," Connie said. She counted them. "Eleven."

"Think they're the treasure?" Nelli asked.

Bones carefully took the pouch and examined it

while Maddock examined the cavity, pressing and digging with his fingers at the sandstone within.

"Need a boost, Maddock?"

When Maddock didn't offer a retort, Bones began examining the brittle leather more closely. "Looks pretty old," he said. "At least a century, maybe more."

"Nothing else in here," Maddock said, scrutinizing the area around the cavity with a practiced eye. "I think you're right, Connie. This was probably hidden for a very long time. In any case, visitors' hands, moisture freezing and thawing, the wind and rain slowly eroded the sandstone. My guess would be that someone would've discovered it in the next few weeks."

He began taking photos with his cell phone, of the cavity, the path the eroding rain water continued to take, the rock sitting in the puddle below, and finally the pouch and arrowheads.

"Is eleven an important number to Native American beliefs?" Nelli asked Bones. "Do you think they're ceremonial?"

"Only if you're playing craps at an Indian casino." Bones picked up and examined one of the arrowheads closely, wondering at its purpose. "These must have been ceremonial."

"I'm not aware of any significant sources of turquoise in Ohio," Nelli said.

Connie asked, "Doesn't most of it come from out west?"

Nelli pursed her lips, thinking. "I remember something about turquoise mines or something like that in Pennsylvania."

Connie looked at her sister with a raised eyebrow.

Defensively, Nelli said, "You know I got my M.B.A.

at Penn State. Just one of those useless facts I heard somewhere."

As Bones examined the arrowheads, he realized something was very wrong.

"These don't look right," he said.

"What's that?" Maddock asked.

"Forget the turquoise. These arrowheads aren't shaped like any Native American points I've ever seen. Not that I know them all, but still." He held one out for Maddock to inspect.

The deep, blue stone was finely crafted, beveled along the edges and coming to a fine point. It lacked a stem. Nor did it have side or corner notches where the arrowhead would be affixed to the shaft. Instead, a single, deep notch was cut into the base, just the right width for the shaft to be fitted in.

"It's almost like a Lanceolate point," Bones said, "but those just have a small, shallow notch here." He pointed to the base. "And see how this curved in on either side?"

Maddock nodded. "It almost looks like a claw."

"Right. Lanceolate points aren't usually shaped like that. They usually curve outward at the base, almost like a fish's tail." He scratched his head. "And the craftsmanship of these things. They're refined. I don't think they were made for everyday use."

Maddock turned the arrowhead over in his hand. His eyes went wide.

"And this isn't turquoise. It's lapis lazuli."

Bones knew his friend was correct. "Holy crap, you're right," he said, feeling foolish. "I was so focused on the shape I didn't think about the material. That makes them seem even more…alien."

"Where is lapis lazuli mined?" Nelli asked.

"Anywhere in the States?"

"A couple places out west in very small quantities," Maddock said. "But mostly it comes from Afghanistan. It was common in some parts of the ancient world. Egypt, for example. They used it on King Tut's funeral mask. But it didn't even reach Europe until the Middle Ages."

"This is weird," Nelli said. "What do we do with them? Put them back?"

Maddock shook his head. "We can't leave the pouch and arrowheads here. Now that their hiding place has been uncovered, someone would come along and take them."

"We're in a state park," Nelli warned. "We could get arrested. Fined or worse."

"Only if we get caught." Thinking of Tam Broderick, with her CIA and law enforcement connections, Bones added, "We know somebody who can help us out if we get into a tight spot; as long as it's not too tight."

"You do this all the time?" Connie asked.

The same time Maddock said, "Not all the time," Bones said, "Pretty much."

Bones took the arrowheads from Connie and slipped them back into the pouch.

"I've got a plastic bag in my drawstring bag," Connie said, sliding it off. "If we got caught out in the rain too long, I was going to put my and Nelli's cell phones in it."

"Okay," Maddock said. "You carry the arrowheads. Let's get going."

Bones slid the pouch into Connie's plastic bag. "Where to?"

"Storm's letting up," Maddock said. "I think we found whatever treasure there is to find."

Bones thought about the ghosts. "Maddock, who do

you think hid those arrowheads? Maybe those two brothers or the hermit or someone is buried around here? I'm feeling lucky. Why don't we look for a burial site?"

The two ladies looked at Maddock with pleading faces. Bones stood between them and rested a hand on each of their shoulders. "You that excited about hopping back in that dinky car?"

"There are two waterfalls down that way," Connie said, pointing southwest. "Even if we don't find anything, we've come this far. Why not get the full tour?"

7

The four explored Lower Falls and then made their way down the trail and stairs to Broken Rock Falls. The falls were small and not very wide or torrential, despite the added flow from the day's rain. Beyond that, nothing in the surrounding area suggested a potential grave.

Admiring the scenery and thinking about what tomorrow might bring, Maddock's eyes moved one more time to the waterfall. "I have an idea." He paused, assessing the rocks along the waterfall again. "It's a cliché but wouldn't be the first time."

Bones, one boot resting on a log twenty feet to Maddock's left, looked puzzled. Then understanding dawned in his eyes.

Once again they looked for a place that wouldn't be too difficult to carry a body to, and focused on places that weren't too high. They climbed Broken Rock Falls' stone steps. Connie and Nelli watched with interest and began to follow the two determined men.

Neither Maddock nor Bones saw anything. Broken Rock Falls and Lower Falls were smaller than Upper Falls, and all three were just too small to really conceal what they were looking for. But Maddock, in the lead, climbed off to the left, not ready to give up.

The crevices, ledges and overhangs, and the porous sandstone walls offered little challenge, despite their dampness.

Then Maddock observed the base of a small shrub emerging from the cliff face. It was perched between the regular sandstone and another rock, one just a shade darker. Along its right side was a finger-width gap, hidden by the foliage, and possibly formed when the stem of the stout shrub thickened over the past couple of years.

"Check this out, Bones," he said and climbed in front of the discolored rock. He ran his fingers inside and along the gap.

"You got that intense look going on, Maddock," Bone said, climbing over next to his friend. "Like when you're massaging a plumber's crack."

Nearby, on the steps, Nelli giggled while Connie groaned at the comment.

"The rock is over four inches thick." Maddock repositioned himself to get better leverage. He pushed, then pulled, trying to dislodge the stone. Then he tried tugging to the right. It budged a quarter of an inch, and stopped.

"Whoa," Bones said, placing a hand in the widened gap. "You're going to need some real man strength if you want to get that opened."

"Okay," Maddock said. "You'd better climb down and find someone who can help me, then."

That time Connie laughed and Nelli groaned.

Both men gave it all they had. Muscles bulged and sinews strained until the rock shifted back an inch. A moment later their efforts managed to shove it aside, revealing a cave just big enough to crawl into.

Maddock shined his Maglite inside. It looked deep, curving left and sloping upward. "Bingo."

"Did someone bring their grandma?" Bones asked.

Maddock crawled in first, Maglite clenched between his teeth. Bones followed.

Initially it was a little tight for the oversized

Cherokee's shoulders, but the tunnel widened as it sloped upward. Nelli and Connie followed on his heels.

"No one's been in here in a long time," he said. "Usually caves, unless they're regularly maintained, are filled with debris—beer bottles, cigarette butts."

The tunnel leveled out and straightened before narrowing. Maddock's flashlight fell upon a blank wall ahead. He was about to declare a dead end when he realized the cave took a sharp left. Making the turn he discovered a small chamber.

Panning his flashlight around before crawling in, he determined it was roughly ten feet across, nearly as wide, and tall enough to sit in. Well, maybe Bones would have to hunch over a little.

The chamber was featureless, no shelves or anything carved into the walls, ceiling or floor, and showed no residual evidence of soot from fires. As with the tunnel leading in, the air was stuffy and stale, but not damp as Maddock expected it would be. Beyond that, the space was dry, which seemed unusual for a large cavity surrounded by such porous rock. That wasn't the only thing unusual. Maddock made way for Bones, keeping his Maglite focused on a skeleton tucked against the far wall, one wrapped in tattered blankets.

Both Maddock and Bones crawled closer to the human remains.

Maddock took the flashlight from his mouth. "No other exit."

Bones quickly flashed his light about, confirming his partner's assertion.

Mummified skin lay stretched across the skeleton, but with wide gaps. Scattered tufts of hair indicated that, in life, the man sported both long hair and a lengthy beard.

Bones kept the two ladies back while Maddock took several photos with his cell phone.

The moldering bits of clothing were even less intact than the blankets.

"This looks more like a tomb than a burial chamber," Connie said, trying to come to terms with what they'd discovered.

Panning along the walls with her keychain flashlight, Nelli added, "Maybe this is where he came to die. What do you think, Bones?"

Maddock moved closer for a better look. "No, he was murdered." He pointed to a deep compression in the skull. "Someone brought him here and killed him…maybe not in that order."

"Think he died to protect the secret of the arrowheads?" Bones asked, sounding doubtful. He crawled up next to Maddock and pulled back the blankets.

Both girls shied away, Connie gasping, while Nelli whispered, "Gross."

"Holy crap!" Bones said. "Look at this."

Most of the man's flesh had long ago rotted away, and lying on the spinal column was the oddest looking ring Maddock had ever seen. It appeared to be an oversized, flat disk made of lead with a raised image on its surface.

Bones leaned closer, adding his light to his friend's. "Maddock, that's identical to the petroglyph I spotted below Rock House."

"That guy must've had big fingers," Nelli said. "Bones, that'd fall off your thumb."

Maddock thought a moment. "It's not a ring. It's a

key."

Bones grinned. "The old hermit dude must've swallowed it to keep it from his killers."

"What's it a key to?" Connie whispered.

They all exchanged glances before Nelli asked Maddock and Bones, "Do you guys know?"

"Seems like another mystery," Maddock replied. "Hopefully some archaeologist will be able to figure it out." He took a quick picture with his cell phone. "Bones and I will hang around while you ladies go and report the find. Now that it's open, can't risk someone else coming upon it."

Connie asked, "What should we say?"

"Just keep it simple," Maddock explained. "Found an opening in the rock. Climbed in and found the skeletal remains. Thought it should be reported."

After both ladies nodded understanding, it was time to crawl back out.

Maddock emerged first, Connie trailing behind. Immediately he sensed something was wrong. His gut was right. Three armed men, Native Americans, stood below, looking up at him. All three wore brown leather duster jackets, the kind associated with the Old West. The oldest of the three, standing in the middle, held a revolver casually pointed up at Maddock. Probably a .45 caliber, and single-action, as he had the hammer cocked.

Prominent crow's feet and deep frown lines framed the no nonsense man's weathered face.

The other two men, possibly the old man's sons by their looks and similar long hair, probably in their forties, each held a semi-automatic pistol. Theirs were casually pointed at the ground. A quick glance suggested they were Colt 1911 ACPs. Old school, just not as old school as their father's.

The old man spoke. "I want the four of you to come on out of there, slowly, and join us down here." His voice, filled with calm confidence, carried over the noise of the nearby falls crashing down on the rocks.

Maddock made a quick assessment of the situation. Because of their propensity for run-ins with groups like the Dominion and the Trident, he had his Walther and knew Bones was carrying his Glock. But they were at a severe disadvantage, and they had two inexperienced ladies to consider. These guys didn't fit the Dominion profile, nor the Trident one. Besides, there was nothing in the cave behind him worth getting into a gunfight over. He spoke back over his shoulder. "Come out slowly. We have at least three armed men interested in talking to us." At least, he hoped talking was all the old man and his sons intended.

While Maddock and Connie began their descent, Bones emerged and eyed the three men before moving out onto the ledge with the skill of a mountain goat. He waited fifteen seconds before shooting the old Native American an apologetic glance. He then stuck his head back into the cave's mouth and signaled Nelli to come out. He said to the old man, "Some people get shy when guns might be pointed their direction."

The old Native American nodded but didn't lower his revolver.

A few seconds later Nelli emerged, breathing hard, with a look of concern on her face. After she and Bones descended without incident, the old man signaled them with the barrel of his revolver to stand next to Maddock and Connie. The four stood with their backs to the shallow, fast-moving stream. One of the brothers stood off to their right, keeping an eye on them.

Maddock took the time to look around. It was only these three, and it didn't appear any visitors to the park were nearby. The old man looked serious, but he didn't have the eyes of a cold-blooded killer. If he and Bones went along, nobody would get hurt, including the three Native Americans.

The brother standing off to the side half shouted, "Did you find the hermit in there?"

With an uncaring voice, Bones asked, "Why don't you see for yourself?"

The old man gazed at Bones. "You are one of us, but have no respect for our history and culture."

"No natives in the cave," Bone said, tilting his head toward the opening. "Only what's left of some old white dude."

The other brother standing next to the old man smirked. "Give us the treasure."

"Yeah," said the other brother, the one standing off to their right,

"Does it look like we're carrying treasure?" Bones asked.

Maddock spread his arms to emphasize the point.

"Relax," the old man told his son. Then he said to the four, mainly focusing on Maddock and Bones, "The hermit stole a Native American treasure—nothing large, but it's important."

Bones glared at the excited son. "What's so important about it?"

The son glared back.

Maddock and Bones looked at one another and nodded. Maddock said to Connie, "Give them the pouch."

Obeying without hesitation, she started to unsling her string bag, and Maddock warned her, watching the excited son. "Slowly."

Connie's eyes widened, realizing her mistake, and cautiously knelt, resting her string bag on the muddy ground. Slowly she opened it and withdrew the plastic bag holding the pouch and arrowheads. She handed it up to Maddock, who stepped forward to hand it to the old man.

The old Native American signaled with his gun's barrel for Maddock to give the bag to his son standing on his left.

"That's a nice six-shooter," Bones said to the old man. He'd had a gun pointed at him more times than he cared to count. Being himself would help the girls realize the situation isn't as deadly as it might appear to them. Sure, things could go sour on a dime, but he trusted Maddock to keep that from happening.

The son holstered his pistol and examined the plastic bag's contents. After doing so, he said with a pleased smile, "Turquoise arrowheads. Eleven of them." No one corrected him.

The old man frowned. "Are you sure that's all?"

Bones said, "Of course it is."

The old man's left eye squinted as he appraised each of them in turn. He took the arrowheads from his son and slipped them into his dust jacket's pocket. "Check them."

Maddock figured if they checked his phone for pictures, they wouldn't find anything out of line. The last picture he took was of the key. That artifact was still in the cave, theirs to find.

The son from their right frisked each of them. He

pulled Maddock's Walther, and Bones' Glock and knife, but found nothing else of interest.

"Remove the bullets from their magazines and give the guns back," the old man said.

With assured familiarity, the son did as directed. "The knife?"

"Give it back to him," the old man replied. When the weapons had been returned, the old man scowled at them. "Go, and leave the park."

The four backtracked, making their way to Nelli's Jeep Wrangler. "Guess that answers who was following us," Maddock said, once they were out in the open, crossing the road leading to the parking lot. He considered making a call from the Visitor Center. They had to have a land line. But contacting the park rangers wouldn't make any difference. There'd be too many questions to answer, and anything of value was already long gone.

"Give me the keys," Maddock said. "I'll drive."

Once they'd pulled onto State Route 664, heading back toward Conkle's Hollow where the rental car was parked, Nelli let out a huge sigh. Maddock saw her eyes sparkle as she smiled.

Sitting next to Maddock, Bones grinned even wider, like the Cheshire Cat. Connie looked puzzled, but Maddock was beginning to suspect. When Nelli unbuttoned her shirt, he was sure. Within seconds she plucked the lead key from her ample cleavage and handed it up to Bones.

The only words her little sister could manage were filled with admiration. "No way."

Bones asked Nelli, "Girl, what made you think to go back and get the key?"

"Maddock's voice," she said, with a sheepish grin. "Whoever was out there, I knew it wasn't park rangers. Whoever it was would steal it. Better that we take it before they got the chance. Right?"

"Nice job," Bones said. "You only made one mistake."

"Oh, what's that?"

"You should have let me pluck it out for you."

8

The park was deserted when Maddock and Bones returned beneath the cover of darkness. Further research had uncovered an account of treasure being hidden in a small recess on a cliff face in Conkle's Hollow and marked the spot by carving an arrow in the stone. According to the story, the Native Americans who hid the treasure had reached the recess by climbing a tree, but when they returned months later, a storm had knocked the tree down, and attempts to reach the spot had failed.

They decided if there ever was a treasure there, it was long gone. Maddock concluded that without a tree, they'd use a rope and lower someone down the cliff to retrieve it. Bones added that, "Only white dudes would need an arrow to remind them where they'd hid their treasure."

With that, the pair of experienced treasure hunters finished their research and plotted their post-midnight excursion.

The three-quarters moon in the nearly cloudless night sky, the warm front that brought with it dry air, and the fact that there wasn't a child to rescue, changed things. It moved the climb down the cliff face below the west end of Rock House from very challenging to moderately difficult, for them. Close to impossible without ropes and tackle for just about anyone else.

Maddock remembered the route Bones had descended to rescue Billy, and approximately how far down he was when he exclaimed, "Holy crap!" Still, it took him a minute to locate the petroglyph. The fact that it was in a recess, with some vines and moss growing over it, left the carving mostly obscured. Add to that the fact that that particular part of the wall was angled away from the main trail, no wonder it hadn't been found.

Once Maddock spotted the petroglyph, Bones moved closer and cleaned it with his knife. When he finished, their eyes met. Clinging to the rock like a spider, Bones slid his knife back into its sheath and pulled the key from his pocket.

"You found it," Maddock said. "You can do the honors."

Bones took a moment to examine the petroglyph before pressing the key into its center and twisting.

With a scraping sound, the petroglyph turned counter clockwise before a stone plug screwed out. Maddock used his Maglite to illuminate a narrow, hollowed out shaft that plunged deep into the rock.

Bones spotted the beam's light reflecting off something shiny inside. He pulled his knife again, and carefully prodded, being wary of traps. There were none. After sheathing his knife, Bones reached in. Maddock whistled as he withdrew an exquisitely crafted compound bow. It was made of polished horn and dark, lacquered wood, and tipped in gold at both ends. The grip was colored bright blue.

"This is wild," Bones said. "Look at the shape, like a flattened 'W.' There's no way this was made by any tribe around here." He handed the bow to Maddock, who examined it carefully.

"The grip almost looks like it's colored with powdered azurite."

"That isn't all." Bones withdrew another object--a golden arrow tipped with a lapis lazuli point. The feathers were white with black on the edges.

"Those look like ibis feathers," Maddock said slowly. Native to Africa and the Middle East, the Ibis was held sacred by the Egyptians for its connection to the god Thoth. "Which means that arrow probably wasn't crafted anywhere in the Americas."

"Well, we know it's not impossible that Egyptians came to this part of the world," Bones said, remembering a particular discovery they had made many years before.

"Yes, but that was a very specific set of circumstances and probably isolated."

"Well, check this out," Bones said, holding the arrow to better show the symbols running down the shaft.

"Hieroglyphs! Here, hold it still," Maddock said, before placing his Maglite in his mouth and pulling out his cell phone to take a series of photographs. It would've been an impossible task for most men. But, considering rock climbing skills, and much more, neither Maddock nor Bones were 'most men.'

"What do you think we should do with it?" Bones asked.

"Put them back," Maddock said. "We'll get this key to that visiting professor Connie mentioned, along with instructions."

"Don't tell the girls?"

Maddock shook his head. "It might cause them to run afoul of those three we met earlier. People know you climbed down here to save that boy. As for the key? Who says we didn't just find it here?"

Bones nodded in agreement before placing the arrow back into its home. How long had it been there?

Maddock figured he could give his sister Avery a heads up, to watch for pictures and publications about its 'discovery' in newspapers and scholarly journals.

"It's a shame to leave it behind," Bones said. "Sort of feels both wrong and right."

After closing everything up and Bones returned the key to his pocket, Maddock took one more photo, a quick one of the petroglyph, then slid his cell phone back into his pocket. "We found it first, Bones. Nothing will ever change that. It's what we do."

"It's not the only thing we do, Maddock."

"True. I want to follow up on this. If Egyptians came to this part of the Americas…"

"Not that. I mean rock climbing." Bones' wide grin captured the slivers of moonlight. "Race you to the top."

9

The Great Serpent Mound was situated atop a plateau among the rolling hills and lush forests of rural Adams County, Ohio. From its curled tail, the four foot high monument wound its way through a manicured carpet of green, its sinuous coils doubling back on one another again and again until it reached the oval head, a quarter of a mile away. Maddock and Bones strode along the path that encircled the monument, taking in the scene.

"I thought it would be bigger," Maddock said.

"That's what my sister said the first time you two hooked up."

Maddock rolled his eyes. He and Bones' sister, Angel, had been engaged, but they were no longer together. The thought didn't exactly pain him, but it felt wrong, like ghost pain from a lost limb. He shook his head and focused on the Serpent Mound. The sight was impressive, but he'd always envisioned something taller, like the Indian mounds of the southeast.

"It's actually the largest serpent effigy in the world." A woman in a park ranger uniform approached. She was short, with fair skin and big, cornflower blue eyes. She wore her blonde, almost white, hair in a single braid. Maddock guessed her to be in her late twenties. She was also exactly the person they were looking for.

"I'm Pari," she said.

"I'm Maddock, this is Bones."

Pari flashed a bright smile. "I'm guessing those are not your actual first names?"

"No. Dane and Uriah."

Bones let out a grunt. He didn't care for his name.

"Dane and Uriah," Pari tapped her chin thoughtfully. "I think I'd go with a different name, too. Just kidding," she added hastily, reaching out and touching Maddock's forearm.

"No worries," Maddock said.

"Pari, that is a beautiful name," Bones said, shouldering his way past Maddock. "What does it mean?"

"It's an Indian name. It means beauty." She glanced away as she spoke.

"Aptly named. Your mother must have had the gift of prophecy."

Maddock let out a laugh that his fake cough didn't quite cover.

"No. It just means my mother was superficial as hell." She took a step to the side and focused her attention on Maddock. "How can I help the two of you?"

"What else can you tell us about the mound?" Given the touchy subject he and Bones planned to broach, it was probably best to give the ranger a chance to warm to them first. It would help if Bones stopped hitting on her.

"Well, it's over thirteen hundred feet long. The height varies, ranging from roughly four to five feet. Based on recent radiocarbon analysis, it's estimated that the mound dates to 321 BCE, one year after the death of Aristotle."

"What's up with the shape of its head?" Bones asked, pointing at the large oval up ahead of them.

"It's an unusual design," Pari agreed. "Some say the oval represents an enlarged eye while others believe it's something being swallowed by the jaws of the serpent."

"Which side do you come down on?" Maddock asked.

"A lidar scan of the mound was done a few years ago. The resulting image looks, to me, like a serpent swallowing an egg. You can actually see it inside the visitor's center."

Maddock assured her they would check it out. As they continued talking, Pari warmed to her subject. She filled them in on a variety of details. Unlike other mounds in the area, Serpent Mound concealed neither graves nor artifacts, suggesting that it was constructed for an atypical purpose.

"The layout of the mound actually matches up with the constellation Draco. The first curve below the head aligns with the star Thuban, which was used as the 'north pole star' during the time the mound was built. This suggests it might be some sort of compass, pointing toward true north."

"That's cool," Bones said. "You know, the Egyptians built the pyramids to align with Orion's belt."

"I did know that," she said. "Egyptology is sort of my hobby."

"That's actually the reason we're here," Maddock said, "although we really were interested in the mound. We're investigating a legend regarding ancient Egyptians reaching the Americas. Specifically, this part of the country."

"We're not nutjobs," Bones said. "A friend of yours sent us."

Pari blanched, then cleared her throat. "Kelli sent you?"

Maddock frowned, wondering if he'd misheard her. "Nelli. She said you two are related."

Her posture relaxed and she let out the breath she'd been holding. "Just checking. You're not the first to pay me a visit today. The other guys were, I don't know, sketchy."

"What did they look like?" Maddock asked.

"One had big sideburns, like late 70's Elvis. The other was kind of thick set, wore a suit," Pari rolled her eyes, "and no tie. Top buttons undone, gold necklace, smoker. Total douche. Anyway, Nelli had texted to let me know she'd sent a couple of people my way, but she didn't describe who would be coming, except..." She paused in midsentence.

"Except what?" Bones asked, grinning.

"Nothing. I misspoke." Her crimson cheeks told a different story. She looked around. "Follow me." She led them a short distance away from the mound, out into an open space, just far enough to be out of earshot of any visitors walking the path around the Great Serpent. "Sorry if I'm acting weird, but those guys who came buy have me feeling a little out of sorts."

"It's not a problem," Maddock said. "We're just grateful you're willing to talk to us."

"I don't know how much I can really help you. It's not like I can tell you anything definitive. It's more a legend that's been passed down in my family."

"That's cool," Bones said. "We prefer legends that haven't been spread all over the internet. That way, if there's something legit there, it's less likely to have been discovered."

Pari nodded. "The story passed down to me is that one of my many-greats grandfathers discovered a treasure somewhere on our family's land. He wasn't sure what, exactly it was, except that it appeared to be ancient and from another part of the world. This was a long time ago and he had no expertise in such things. But he gathered a few items before something spooked him."

"What was it?" Maddock asked.

"All he ever said was there was an evil spirit down there."

Maddock slowly nodded. As evidence went, the story was paper thin.

"What makes you think the treasure might have been Egyptian?" he asked.

"A piece of it was passed down to me by my Aunt Ruth." Pari unbuttoned the top button of her shirt, and drew out a gold pendant on a leather thong. Maddock recognized it at once.

"An ankh!" The cross shape with a loop at the top was an ancient Egyptian symbol of life.

"I've had it examine by an Egyptologist who believes it's authentic, but he's not certain about the crystal." She flipped the ankh around to reveal a pale blue crystal embedded in the center, between the arms. "This thing is weird, too. It totally jacks up my cellphone if I hold it too close. And it does something weird with light."

Maddock glanced at Bones, thinking the two of them already knew what Pari was about to tell them.

"I know it makes no sense, but if you expose it to even a small amount of light, the crystal seems to take the light in and amplify it. I can take it into a pitch-black room, strike a match in front of the crystal, hold it for a few seconds, and the crystal glows like a flashlight and keeps glowing for several minutes. I can show you right now, if you like."

"We believe you," Maddock said. "In fact, we've actually seen a few crystals like this before."

"Seriously? Where?"

Maddock knew that it probably wouldn't be a good idea to start talking about Atlanteans, so he opted for a version of the truth. "In some ancient world sites. They're exceedingly rare, and as I'm sure you know, their properties are so... otherworldly that reputable scientists wouldn't want to risk their reputations by discussing their findings."

Pari let out a long, slow breath, her posture visibly relaxed. "You have no idea how good it feels to be able to talk about this and have someone believe me who isn't a stoner or a new age hippie."

"And that was found on your family's property?" Bones asked.

"That's the way the story goes. Officially the location was kept secret, but my Aunt Ruth hinted that it was passed down through the generations." She shrugged.

"Would it be possible for us to speak with your aunt?" Maddock asked.

Pari hesitated, then nodded. "Nelli said you're good guys, and that you stood up for an elderly couple who was being harassed. Right now, I think Aunt Ruth could do with somebody standing up for her."

"What do you mean?" Bones asked.

"It's actually about the treasure. Certain members of the family think she's concealing the secret and they're making life miserable for her. I've told them to leave her alone, which is pretty much the full extend of what I'm able to do."

"We'll certainly do our best," Maddock said.

"Only if you're sure you don't mind dipping your toe into turbulent waters. These guys have a reputation as local bullies, but you two look like you can handle yourselves."

Bones flashed a broad grin. "Are they rednecks? Please say they're rednecks."

10

The state highway wound through the rural countryside. Bones stretched his nearly six-foot-six frame within the rented white SUV and turned to Maddock.

"You about done counting barns?"

Maddock shot a confused, blue-eyed glance at his friend. "What are you talking about?"

"We're over an hour northeast of Wright Patterson Air Force Base, cruising past the thirty-seventh barn. I figure you've given up on the treasure hunt and are scoping out the farmer's daughters."

Maddock smirked. "You must've dozed off. We're up to thirty-nine barns."

"Not my fault. You were listening to Gordon freaking Lightfoot. I didn't know anyone actually owned his music."

"Hey, my dad loved Gordon Lighfoot."

"And that's fine for your dad. But you aren't old enough for the early bird special at iHop, no matter how hard you try to act like a grandma."

"This should help." Maddock disconnected his phone from the car stereo, turned on the radio, and scanned the channels until he found a country station. It was one of those generic, modern country songs, a random male singing about his girl, his truck, and the moonlight.

Bones covered his ears. "I surrender. You know my Kryptonite." He reached over and scanned over to a hard rock station. "The only country music I'll listen to is

Willie Nelson, mostly because dude knows how to party, and that one by David Allan Coe."

Maddock chuckled as he took the SUV into a curve cut into a hillside. "We're almost there."

Bones glanced at the sign. "Podunkville, Ohio. Population, Maddock's IQ—holy crap!"

The warning came a fraction of a second after Maddock perceived the oncoming danger. Some idiot in a red pickup truck was in his lane, trying to pass a Chevy Cruze.

Travelling at 60 miles per hour, Maddock evaluated his options in a fraction of a second: Slam on the brakes and hope to survive the head-on impact. Veer right and almost certainly descend into a rollover crash ending either against one of the stout maples littering the steep hillside, or settling in the soybean field sixty feet below. Or the only viable option.

Maddock cut left, crossing in front of the oncoming Cruze. The sedan missed the Ford Explorer's rear bumper by inches. Belatedly the Cruze's driver slammed on his brakes, tires screeched and horn blasted. The red pickup truck didn't even slow down.

Angling his SUV up the hillside, Maddock fought the wheel while the rugged terrain abused both the tires and the front suspension system. Branches slapped against the windshield and driver's side mirror as he threaded the vehicle between a pair of white pines.

Maddock tapped the brakes, hoping the weeds and tangled brambles weren't hiding any fallen logs, boulders or deep furrows. He had another decision to make while maneuvering between a pair of maple saplings. Fifty feet ahead stood a line of pines. He still had too much speed to stop in time. He might be able to fit his vehicle between two of them. But, within thirty feet, the hillside shifted from a thirty to a fifty-degree climb. The rented SUV wasn't a real off-road vehicle, leaving him little confidence his ride could handle it. Realizing his only option, Maddock hauled the wheel back to the right.

His hand clamped on the bouncing vehicle's grab handle, Bones kept quiet. Any suggestions would be useless by the time they reached Maddock's ears. The smart bet was to count on his partner's experience and split-second reactions.

The SUV careened back down the hillside, branches from another pine whipping across the windshield and driver's side mirror. The rough ride and Maddock's judicious use of the brakes had bled off most of the vehicle's speed. That assisted his maintaining control as the vehicle thumped and bounced across the uneven ground near the road's shoulder.

Maddock spotted a blue sports car approaching along the inside lane. He gunned the Explorer's V-6 engine. The car rental agency hadn't had anything more powerful available. Maddock turned the wheel, playing the hand he was dealt. His white Explorer bounded onto the road in front of the blue Camaro. Maddock made it to the original far lane with less than a yard to spare, the SUV's passenger side wheels skidding on the narrow shoulder's gravel.

Bones casually glanced out the window, feeling the vehicle lean heavily to the right, being rather top-heavy for such a maneuver.

The Camaro driver sounded his horn, but continued on his way, nearly rear-ending the Cruze, only beginning to pick up speed.

Maddock regained full control and eased back onto

the state route, stepping on the accelerator.

"Did you opt for the full insurance?" Bones asked. "Because this thing's gonna need detailing and an alignment."

Maddock laughed, feeling the adrenalin rush fade. "Did you get that truck's plate number?"

"No." Bones scowled. "But I did notice that he's a Steelers fan."

Maddock nodded. He'd seen the tattered ball cap through the windshield as well. "More rust than red paint. Probably a dozen in this county just like it."

"So, what do you think the big secret is that Paris' aunt is keeping?"

After passing a Chevy dealership, Maddock braked and flipped on the left turn signal. "I don't know. I just hope she really is willing to share. Otherwise it's been a wasted trip."

Bones observed the sign posted in front of the parking lot where Maddock was turning their SUV into. Mallard Creek Care. A nursing home.

"Behave yourself in there, Maddock. I know that some guys go for cougars, but I think they discourage visitors hooking up with the residents."

11

While Maddock and Bones signed in, hastily scribbling their names, the visitor desk attendant informed them that the residents had just finished breakfast and should be in their rooms, or engaged in one of the morning activities.

Maddock led Bones down a series of tiled floor corridors, following posted signs to reach the nursing home's rehabilitation wing. Pictures of flowers and birds lined the cream-colored walls. The antiseptic smell assaulted Maddock's nose, but it was better than stale urine, a childhood memory that lingered from when his mother took him to visit an ailing neighbor.

Stopping at the nurses' station that appeared to be the hub of three hallways, counting the one they'd traveled down, Maddock asked directions to Ruth Harshbinner's room. A nursing aid pointed down a hallway. "Most everyone's doing crafts or bingo, but Mrs. Harshbinner's in the lounge, reading one of her romance novels."

The lounge area was wide open and lined with windows. On one end of the room sat a walnut console piano. The other side held a matching walnut, five-paned songbird aviary. Maddock estimated it housed at least a dozen colorful finches flitting around from branch to branch. Next to the aviary, a thin, gray-haired woman with hearing aids sat in a wheelchair. She peered through a pair of round spectacles at the pages of a paperback novel. The cover suggested it was a bodice ripper.

After a few seconds the woman in the wheelchair looked up from her book and smiled at Maddock. Her eyes widened a bit after they caught sight of Bones standing behind him. Maddock wasn't short by any means, being just under six feet, but his friend had six inches on him. Both men had retained much of their physiques from their Navy SEAL days.

The old woman said loudly, pointing to herself, "Are you here to see me?"

Maddock saw some of the family resemblance. The woman seated in the wheelchair was Pari's Great Aunt Ruth. "We're here to see you, Mrs. Harshbinner. Your grandniece, Pari, asked us to stop by."

Ruth Harshbinner set aside her paperback and signaled for Maddock to wait. Her hands shook a little as she reached behind each ear and switched on her hearing aids. "Can't concentrate worth two hoots of a horse when people come in here jabbering about nothing or turn on the soap operas." Her eyes narrowed. "You look like the men Pari told me about."

Maddock nodded. "She asked us to stop by."

Ruth's face scrunched up in thought, then nodded once to herself. "Over there by the bookshelves." She flicked her wrist that direction to emphasize. "The birds remind me of the ones that visit my feeder outside my kitchen window, and the bookshelves are like the ones in my sitting room."

Maddock moved behind the wheelchair and pushed it the ten or so feet next to a deep chocolate-colored armchair. He stepped back around and formally introduced himself. "I'm Dane Maddock." He reached forward and shook Ruth Harshbinner's hand. Despite her frail appearance, Mrs. Harshbinner's grip was warm and firm. "And this is my friend." He gestured to Bones.

The tall Cherokee nodded and extended his hand. "Call me Bones."

"Bones?" Ruth asked. "I can see you have Indian heritage. Is that your first name?"

"My friends call me Bones," he said, shaking the elderly woman's hand. "Short for Bonebrake."

The look on Ruth's face told Maddock she sensed something...something that she couldn't quite place her finger on. Dane Maddock knew: His friend hated to be called by his first name, Uriah.

"Pari told me about you two. Said commendable things. But she didn't tell me your Christian name, young man." The old woman squinted up at Bones through her round glasses. "Are you hiding from the law?"

"No, ma'am," Bones said in a serious tone, maintaining eye contact. "No one in the criminal justice system has a warrant for my arrest."

"Oh, that's splendid." Mrs. Harshbinner waved a hand in dismissal. "Everyone should be allowed their secrets." She gestured to an armchair on the far side of the bookcase. "Pull that one up."

Once they were seated, facing each other, Maddock repeated, "Pari asked us to stop by and see you." He paused, then decided to get straight to the point. "She indicated you might have something to share. A family secret that's been causing some problems?"

Ruth Harshbinner raised an eyebrow, then squinted at each of the men. She then looked around to see if anyone else was in the room. Satisfied there wasn't, she said, "Pari is a good girl, a bright girl."

Maddock and Bones nodded.

"A loyal girl," Mrs. Harshbinner continued. A sneer curled the older woman's upper lip. "Unlike my grandson, Gordon. Takes after his father."

Mrs. Harshbinner rubbed her palms on her slacks before pulling her pink sweater tight around her shoulders. "Are you young men good at keeping a secret?"

"Yes," Maddock said. "We are."

"Most definitely," Bones agreed.

The old woman's face ran through several emotions before settling on resignation. "Well, Mr. Maddock and…Bones, even though we haven't known each other long enough to be friends, you appear to be honest." She frowned, solidifying her decision. "I'll have to trust you, and Pari's judgment. She wouldn't have sent you if you weren't reliable." She held out her hands, palms up, a gesture of giving up, of surrender. "I'm clean out of options."

She glanced around the room conspiratorially before continuing. "I am in here, rehabbing after a little heart surgery. A bad valve needed fixing." Her face turned sour. "But, if my son has anything to say about it, here I'll stay."

"Why is that?" Maddock asked. The woman was in a wheelchair, but looked strong enough to walk, if she wanted to. She didn't appear to be mentally deficient or unstable. He was certain it had something to do with the treasure, but wanted her to get around to the topic in her own time.

"My son, Johnny," she said. "He found some fancy new lawyer, or maybe it was the other way around. For my surgery, I gave Johnny my medical power of attorney. Never did fully trust him, but he's the only family left in the nearest three counties."

"If you're recovering, and the legal authority was temporary," Maddock said, "his lawyer will have nothing to stand on."

"Your arrival just might be a godsend," she said to Maddock and Bones. "Johnny now says I'm mentally unstable. His fancy lawyer is bringing in their own psychiatrist to test me." She scowled while her hands balled into fists. "Those head doctors, it's all their highfalutin opinion. Even this old grandma knows how opinions can be bought, even fancy ones."

Maddock's gaze met her teary eyes. "Why would your son do that?"

"He wants the farm." She threw her hands up, frustration filling her voice. "Don't know why. He never wanted to farm. Runs a print shop in town. Does jobs for most everyone in the county. Makes enough money for a vacation home in Florida." A smirk crossed her face. "Audra, his wife, stays there over the winter, which means it's an investment in *his* mental health."

Maddock pondered, the way Mrs. Harshbinner's emotions swung, might she be unstable? Or simply distraught over her son's betrayal?

A stern look formed on Ruth Harshbinner's face. She signaled Maddock and Bones closer. "Johnny doesn't know the secret. What's beneath the fields of our farm..." Her voice trailed off, becoming almost a whisper. "My farm, since Harvey passed." Determination in her voice returned. "But, he suspects something. Our family has tried to keep the legend a secret, even from members of the extended family, but some things, even if unspoken, never fully die down, like tales of my father's so-called Digging Diary."

Ruth glanced around again, then pointed to Bones. "Reach behind those dusty encyclopedias. Pari brought it to me. Hid it there. Left a fake one Harvey wrote decades ago in the lock box on the mantle. He called it his decoy."

Bones felt behind the red and silver 1985 edition of the *Funk & Wagnalls Encyclopedia* and retrieved a leather-bound book. It was the size of his hand and thick as two of his fingers. The brown leather was cracked with age. He guessed time had yellowed the pages as well. "Maddock's got a diary like this," he said. "Except his is pink and came with a fuzzy pen."

A grin split Ruth's face. "Pari told me about you two. Maddock, the serious one and the big fellow always cracking jokes." She made eye contact with each man. "But both professional treasure hunters." She nodded at the diary Bones held. "There's all you need to know."

"I assume this," Maddock held up the diary, "is connected to the treasure Pari told us about?"

Ruth nodded. "I shouldn't have given Pari that old cross, or whatever you call it. It was stupid of me. That's what made Johnny curious."

"You'd like for us to find the treasure before Johnny does?" Bones asked.

"Find it, maybe even destroy it, just keep it away from him."

"Why destroy it?" Maddock asked.

"Harvey got to reading this journal and started poking around. He came in late one night shaking like a leaf in a windstorm, white as a bleached sheet. He said he'd found the entrance, whatever that meant, but he was going to seal it up."

"What did he see?" Bones asked.

She swallowed hard. "It was my uncle," she said, voice dropping to a whisper. "His ghost. After that day Harvey never went to the Hilltop Barn after sunset.

"I saw him too, my uncle's ghost. Twice, holding a glowing lantern. And that's why Johnny thinks he can prove me mentally troubled." She stared at them. "Do you think I'm crazy?"

"No, Ma'am. Bones and I have seen enough of the world to know that everything can't be fully explained."

"Mrs. Harshbinner," Bones began, "are you saying the treasure is hidden under your barn?"

"Read the journal," she said. "Open the book, young man."

Maddock gently lifted the cover. Scrawled on the first page was a small, meticulous script whose coloration and structure suggested use of a dip pen, a precursor to the fountain pen. That helped confirm the diary's age.

"Open to the middle," she said.

He looked up from reading the first page and did as Mrs. Harshbinner directed. The left-hand page he opened to contained more of the meticulous script. The right, a small map, what looked like a branching cave, with small arrows and notations. That wasn't what caught Bones' attention. A square, slightly larger than an inch square had been cut into the pages, forming a hollowed area within the closed journal. The action had removed a portion of each page's words. The loss of content was more than made up by what was cradled within the carved-out portion. There rested a crystal, a type that Maddock recognized.

He lifted it out to show his friend.

Maddock recognized it immediately. He'd seen its

like before, light blue, square, and faceted with perfect clarity, the type they'd found that powered the ancient Atlantis machines.

Bones handed it to Maddock. It lacked the internal spark of light, which meant its energy had been discharged.

Mrs. Harshbinner asked, "You recognize what it is?"

"We've seen this type of crystal before," Maddock replied. "They're extremely rare."

"My father took it to university professors in New York City, and even reputable jewelers. Not one could identify it. Despite their pleas and offers of money, my father wouldn't give it up. Even though those were more honest times than today, my father and uncle traveled under false names and quietly returned home, to the farm. They found that cross of Pari's too. It had a crystal in it like that one. They kept on digging until my uncle disappeared. It's in the—"

She stopped in mid-sentence and looked toward the entrance. A scowl crossed her face.

Maddock pocketed the crystal and Bones closed the journal.

A lanky man with wind-strewn brown hair stood in the entryway. Dark circles lined his bulbous eyes, and his prominent Adam's Apple bobbed as he swallowed. Maddock thought, if anyone were to ever play Ichabod Crane, it was this guy, with his tan overcoat and russet bowtie.

The man's gaze moved from Ruth to Maddock and Bones, followed by a smile creasing his face, one that didn't reach his eyes. "Mother," he said, striding forward. "The nurses' station wasn't sure where you'd wandered off too."

"Not like I was going anywhere, Johnny. Every door's alarmed, keeping me here, just like you want."

He stopped next to his mother's wheelchair, and looked down at her. "That's not true." Then his attention returned to Maddock and Bones. "Who are these gentlemen? Their names on the visitor log were illegible."

Before Maddock or Bones had a chance to respond, Mrs. Harshbinner said, "Friends of the church."

"Oh," Johnny said. "I don't recall seeing you around town. What church do you attend?"

Bones said, "You might call us missionaries to the world."

Maddock nodded once, affirming his friend's statement.

Johnny's eyes moved down to the journal Bones held at his side in his left hand. "You gentlemen aren't soliciting donations from my mother?" His voice sounded distracted, his interest focused on the cracked leather book.

Bones lifted the book and slapped his right hand atop it. "John, three-sixteen, bro. Just sharing the Word."

Johnny was a couple inches taller than Maddock, which still left him at least three shorter than Bones. He squinted, staring up into the taller man's face. He pulled a business card from his coat's pocket and held it out for Bones. "If you have any intention of acquiring a donation for your travels from my mother, you'll be hearing from our lawyer."

"Your lawyer ain't my lawyer," Ruth said.

"Give the card to my lackey." Bones tipped his head toward Maddock. "He takes care of any paperwork."

Maddock reached for the card with his left hand and

extended his right to shake. "I'm Maddock." He mishandled the card and watched it flutter to the floor before bending over to pick it up. The distraction gave Bones time to slip the journal into his leather jacket's inner pocket.

Bones said, "We'll be on our way, Mrs. Harshbinner. It was a pleasure to meet you."

"Walk with God," Ruth Harshbinner said, reaching out and taking a hold of Bones' hands.

12

Maddock and Bones sat huddled in a corner booth of *The Farmer's Daughter*. The home-style cooking and atmosphere was well targeted at its small-town customer base. They'd hardly touched their daily special, meatloaf sandwiches and beer-battered green beans, which seemed to distress the perky brunette waitress. Both men reassured her everything was perfectly acceptable, and to keep the coffee coming.

While Bones read the journal depicting the dig beneath the Hilltop Barn, carefully turning the pages, and leaving torn bits of napkin as bookmarks, Maddock scoured the internet with his cell phone, trying to discover all he could about Clark Clabberson, Esquire. The business card handed over by Johnny Harshbinner, identifying his lawyer, bore that name, as well as a stylized depiction of a golden trident. The emblem had immediately raised suspicion.

Trident was a secret organization with members embedded at all levels of both government and law enforcement. Maddock and Bones had survived several run-ins with the group. Its interests focused on securing ancient relics and associated technology.

"Not much out there," Maddock said to Bones. "He's got a website with basic information on his practice. Deals mainly in real-estate. Law degree from Boston University and a certified CPA. Has one part-time secretary." Maddock set down his phone and took a sip of coffee. "Only odd thing is Clabberson's practice is located in Cleveland."

"Cleveland," Bones said. "Why would Johnny get a lawyer from Cleveland? That must be two or three hours away."

"Probably not a family friend, or someone with close ties to the area," Maddock said. "Or Mrs. Harshbinner would've mentioned that, instead of calling Johnny's attorney 'his fancy lawyer.'"

Before Maddock could respond, his cell phone vibrated, signaling he'd received a text message. "Pari," he said, reading the text. "She says that her cousin, Johnny, was upset with her great-aunt because she had the locks changed."

He read the next two texts that arrived. "Aunt Ruth has spoken to Rick at the hardware store. He'll give us a set of keys to the house. Wants us to videotape what's beneath the Hilltop Barn. Her great-aunt has a camcorder kept in a cabinet next to the TV."

"Trident." Bones tapped his finger on the table. "If they're involved, they'd tap the nursing home's phones."

Maddock finished his friend's thought, knowing Trident had the resources. "I'll bet that's who paid Pari a visit at the Serpent mound."

"You think she's in danger?"

"They've left her alone. Probably thought she didn't know anything."

"What about the old lady?"

Maddock considered the question. "If they've got Johnny in their pocket, they don't need her."

"And if we uncover this secret before they do, she's out of the crosshairs entirely." Bones closed the diary and slipped it into the pocket of his leather jacket. Around a bite of his cold meatloaf sandwich, he said,

"Let's finish up, hit the hardware store." He swallowed his bite. "Pick up some lights and gear there, and get the keys."

Maddock nodded in agreement. "We should locate Mrs. Harshbinner's camcorder first. We'll probably need to charge its battery."

13

Maddock pulled the rented SUV halfway off the narrow county road just before a culvert bridge, allowing the oncoming semi hauling a good-sized backhoe room to pass. A white work truck followed close behind. Block letters painted on the truck's door said it belonged to Lakeside Star Excavation, based in Cleveland, Ohio.

Staring ahead, Bones said, "Looks like that crew just left our farm."

Maddock waited while a white van pulled out of the farm's gravel driveway and turned left, opposite the direction of the truck.

"Couldn't read the side of the van," Maddock said.

"One word looked like 'Graphic.'" Bones shrugged. "How do they expect to drum up business if people can't read what's on their van?"

"Graphic," Maddock said with a grin. "Bet it belongs to our friend Johnny Harshbinner."

"Follow him?"

Maddock shook his head as he pulled back onto the road. It was already late afternoon. "I'm more interested in Mrs. Harshbinner's farm."

He took the long gravel driveway leading up to the old brick farmhouse. It was two stories, with tall, narrow windows and a porch that encompassed all but the house's west-facing side, opposite the drive. A handful of towering oaks offered shade and a line of white spruce stood to break western winds that might blow across the soybean fields surrounding the house. Two large red barns stood fifty yards behind the home, and about a quarter mile away, atop a sloping rise with a lane running up to it, stood what had to be the Hilltop Barn. It was red as well, but appeared larger than the other two.

Bones pointed to the gray vehicle parked in front of the detached garage next to the farmhouse. Lights, a yellow star, and lettering identified it as belonging to the county sheriff.

"Might explain why Johnny and his excavation crew left," Maddock said, remembering Johnny complaining about his mother changing the locks. He and Bones had permission to be on the property. Might be good to let that fact be known to local law enforcement. If they ran off Johnny's crew, they weren't collaborating with Trident. Or, at least this particular deputy sheriff wasn't.

As it stood, if Trident was involved, odds were they only suspected there might be something of value on the farm property. They wouldn't be fully mobilized. With any luck, he and Bones could get in, find any crystals, videotape for Ruth Harshbinner along the way, and everybody would win. Everybody defined as the good guys. Maddock approached the farmhouse at five miles per hour, allowing the deputy sheriff sitting inside his Ford Crown Victoria to determine he and Bones weren't a threat, despite the fact that they were outsiders to the local community, as evidenced by their rented SUV's plates.

Bones scoffed. "Dude's doing his paperwork."

Maddock shook his head. "Looks like he's on the radio, probably with Dispatch." He pulled their white SUV to a stop about thirty feet away. "Paperwork or radio, it's part of the job."

The deputy stepped out of his vehicle and donned his hat before approaching. Maddock lowered his driver-side window. "Good afternoon, Deputy."

The tall deputy, whose name tag read N. Connors, stopped far enough away that he could observe both Maddock and Bones. Suspicion, more than curiosity or concern, filled the deputy's eyes. "Are you gentlemen lost? Or part of that work crew that just departed?"

"Neither, Deputy," Maddock said with a disarming grin. "We're actually here at Ruth Harshbinner's request."

Despite the brim of the deputy's hat, Maddock spotted the arch of the law officer's left eyebrow. "At Mrs. Harshbinner's request, huh?" Skepticism hung in the question. "Might I ask, what for?"

Maddock sensed his longtime partner's annoyance rising. Nevertheless, being as honest as possible, without revealing Ruth Harshbinner's family secret, seemed the best way to go. "Some video recordings of the property."

"Professional videographers?"

"Not exactly," Maddock replied. The timing of his and Bone's arrival, on the heels of the deputy having to deal with Ruth Harshbinner's son and the excavation crew, was playing against them. "Mrs. Harshbinner had us pick up a set of keys to the new locks at the hardware store. You can call the owner, Rick, to verify." He didn't want the deputy to call Mrs. Harshbinner, not at the nursing home, routing the call through their phone system.

Deputy Collins rubbed his chin. "Gentlemen, please shut off your vehicle and show me your IDs."

Bones frowned. He leaned toward Maddock to speak through the driver's side window. "Ruth got us a set of keys, Bro." He held up the set of house keys. "These say we have permission to be here."

Deputy Collins stood, straight-faced, obviously unfazed by Bones.

Maddock sighed and reached for his wallet. Bones followed suit. The deputy tensed, focused on their movements. Maddock proffered their driver's licenses.

Deputy Collins scrutinized the licenses, comparing the pictures to Maddock and Bones. "Please step out of your vehicle." He gestured over toward the two car detached garage. "Wait over there while I call Mrs. Harshbinner, and verify your story."

While climbing out of the SUV, Maddock said, "Deputy, we picked up the keys from Rick at Lawn Tree Hardware. Wouldn't it be easier to verify through him than trying to track Mrs. Harshbinner down at Mallard Creek?" Using the names of the local establishments couldn't hurt.

The deputy pulled out his cell phone. "Mr. Maddock, Rick doesn't own this property. Ruth Harshbinner does."

Bones grumbled and kicked a few stones in the gravel drive. Both he and Maddock listened to the brief conversation, the entire time the deputy kept his eyes focused on them.

"Yes, it's me again, Mrs. Harshbinner…yes, they're gone…I have two men here, a Dane Maddock and Uriah Bonebrake, from Florida here. They say you want them to do some videotaping of the property…Yes, ma'am, that's the tall fellow's name…"

Bones cursed under his breath, while Maddock grinned up at his friend. Bones hated his first name.

"Understood, Mrs. Harshbinner…Agreed, I hope I don't have to call you again."

The deputy slid his cell into his pocket. "Don't do anything that'll give me or any of my colleagues reason to come back here. And if Mrs. Harshbinner's son, John, shows up, don't get into a confrontation with him, or his lawyer." He pulled a business card from his uniform's shirt pocket and handed it to Bones. "Call us."

Bones grinned. "If Johnny shows up, we'll—"

Maddock cut in, finishing Bone's statement. "—avoid conflict and contact the sheriff's department."

Bones reached over and shoved the card in Maddock's jacket pocket. "Deputy Collins," he said as the law officer turned toward his vehicle.

"Yes, Mr. Bonebrake?"

Bones nodded, indicating the eight-foot-high pile of freshly dug dirt and the associated hole between a pair of white oaks that had to be at least five decades old, maybe more. "What were they doing, digging there?"

The deputy shrugged. "That's where the old outhouse stood."

That explained the pile of broken boards next to the mounds of dirt.

"Holy crap," Bones said. "One big out-of-town backhoe for that?"

Deputy Collins shrugged.

"Why didn't you have them at least fill in the hole before they left?"

"If I ordered them to do that," the deputy explained to Bones, "it would be within their right to bill the sheriff's department for the time and labor. That would vex my boss, and potentially damage any criminal or civil case Mrs. Harshbinner might have against her son."

Bones nodded. "That would be a shit show."

14

For the fifth time, Maddock examined the living room's brick fireplace. It was large, framed by pink granite and, evidenced by soot and remnants of ashes, used, rather than serving solely as an ornamental fixture.

After tapping and pressing on each brick and stone, Maddock again moved to the polished oak mantle, adorned with a cast-iron ring on each end. Upon the decoratively carved wood sat an antique wind-up clock, a small bust, several framed photos, and various painted porcelain knickknacks. He failed to find any keys. No hidden compartments, or anything contained behind, in or under any of the decorations.

For the second time, he moved the clock to an end table, opened its back, and searched for a key hidden among its internal workings.

Bones' attention shifted between his partner's efforts and the false journal he paged through. It'd been stored in a bronze case on the mantle, tucked between the clock Maddock was examining and a small bust of President John F. Kennedy.

"Yo, Maddock." Bones said. "Says in here an unnamed treasure was placed in an iron chest, buried, encased in cement, and an outhouse was constructed over it."

Maddock latched closed the back of the clock and sighed. "Well, that explains what the excavation crew was up to."

Bones tossed the leather-bound false journal to his

partner. "Step aside and let me figure it out while you go see how fast the camcorder is charging."

Ten minutes later, Bones huffed and stepped back from the fireplace. "Johnny Boy must've found the keys and took them."

"That doesn't make sense," Maddock replied, returning the false journal to its case. "Check the authentic journal again. It says 'the mantle holds the keys,' right?"

Bones grunted agreement while rereading the statement and surrounding pages yet again. Fortunately that statement, near the center of the journal, hadn't been partially cut out to make room for the expended crystal.

"This is the only fireplace in the house." Maddock scratched his neck in thought. "Maybe it's not a set of keys in a conventional sense."

Maddock quickly made sure everything on the mantle was back in its place. "Let's go out to the barn and look around while the camcorder charges. Maybe we'll find something out there before the sun sets."

"This place must be the Grand Central Station of Hicksville," Bones said, standing on the farm house's white porch, waiting for Maddock to lock the door.

Maddock pocketed the keys and followed his partner's gaze. An old Chevy pickup, adorned with two parts red paint and one part rust, spewed smoke as it rolled up the long driveway. Two men rode inside and two were sitting in the bed.

"Rednecks," Bones said, no love in his voice. "Seems we've come across that truck once before."

Maddock moved up next to his friend, effectively blocking anyone interested in climbing the steps onto the porch. The split-second view of the truck passing on the hillside curve matched the one approaching them. "I think you're right," he said. "Maybe they're just here to check on Ruth's property while she's convalescing?"

"Sure, Maddock. And Nickelback is my favorite band."

Maddock knew his friend was right. Nothing ever seemed to go easy for them.

The truck skidded on the gravel and came to a halt. The two men in the back, wearing grease and sweat-stained ball caps—one with a Steelers logo—hopped down and pushed the sleeves of their plaid flannel shirts up. They had to be brothers, probably in their early twenties. Two middle-aged men, sporting weather-worn faces covered in beard stubble, stepped out of the truck. The driver scowled while the other spit a stream of tobacco juice onto the grass next to the drive.

Maddock figured the only thing he and Bones had in common with these guys was a preference for jeans and boots, except for they favored grime and grease stains. Any hope of avoiding trouble depended on Maddock saying something before Bones did. His partner hated rednecks, especially unfriendly ones.

"How can we help you?" Maddock began working out a story to explain their presence. It wouldn't have to be complex, just a reason. Estimations for repairs or remodeling? He dismissed that. He and Bones didn't even have a clipboard. The house held a number of old paintings and antique furniture. Claiming to have been appraising them would be good enough. The rednecks probably couldn't tell a Picasso from a paint-by-numbers.

The four locals ambled forward, the driver in the lead. The others spread out, a stride behind their leader who stopped a dozen feet from the porch.

The driver rested his hands on his hips. "Folks around here don't take kindly to trespassers."

Bones inhaled deeply, then crinkled his nose. "Folks around here must not take kindly to deodorant either."

The two younger men balled their fists and stepped forward.

"Bobby, Derek," the driver said, looking at each and raising a hand to stop them. A grin spread across his face. "They're strangers, so we'll cut them a bit of slack." He ignored Bones and focused his gaze on Maddock. "We heard someone was trespassing on Mrs. Harshbinner's property, and we showed up to escort whoever it was off. The way I see it, that would be you two."

"If your source is Johnathan Harshbinner," Maddock said, "he's the one looking at court time for trespassing."

The driver frowned. "Maybe I'll just call the sheriff."

Maddock knew it was a bluff, but the driver's partner didn't and spoke up. "We don't need no deputy to run these two off."

Bobby, the young man on the driver's right wearing the Steelers hat, chimed in. "Yeah, Pa."

Maddock knew where this was going, but wanted to make sure the goons Johnny recruited knew they were in the wrong. He proffered the business card given to him. "Deputy Collins left his card with us earlier. Suggested we call him should we run into any trouble. My guess is he's still on duty."

"Fellows, things around here get settled a lot of ways," the driver said. "Most of them don't involve the law."

All three of the men behind him grinned in anticipation. The driver's partner spit more tobacco juice before adding. "Fellows? That injun's got himself a ponytail. Seems to me he's looking to get one of them Bruce Jenner operations right soon."

Bones grinned. "I would, but then who'd keep your old lady satisfied?"

It took the passenger a few seconds before the smile showing his tobacco-stained teeth turned to a snarl.

Maddock and Bones held their place on the steps, keeping the high ground and ensuring that nobody could get behind them without vaulting onto the railed-in porch.

The tobacco-chewing passenger charged toward Bones while the two younger men ran at Maddock.

Bones drew his fist back as if readying to throw a haymaker, then caught his enraged adversary with a side kick. The man staggered back, clutching his chest, and dropped to the ground like a sack of wheat.

Bones turned to help Maddock.

Whether or not Maddock needed help was debatable. He dodged Bobby's punch, grabbed him by the arm, and used the fellow's momentum to shove him into the second attacker. The two collided hard and landed in a heap on the steps.

Maddock kicked Bobby in the kidney while Bones yanked Derek from the ground. Despite being just over six foot tall and solidly muscled, the farmhand was no match for Bones, who quickly had the man's arm locked behind his back.

Bones asked the driver, "You or any of your asshat friends got any more stupid comments to make?"

The driver reached into his shirt pocket for his cell phone. "Maybe I'll call the sheriff, seeing as how you just assaulted us. Your word against ours, and we know the prosecutor."

Maddock signaled over his shoulder with his thumb toward a window next to the door. "Security camera will tell a different story?" He reached into his jacket pocket. "Would you rather that I make the call?"

The tobacco-chewing man spat out his wad and slowly climbed to his feet. Bobby made it to his knees, grimacing and groaning as his Steelers hat slipped off his head and onto the ground.

Bones let go of Derek and shoved him into the tobacco chewer. The older man had time to brace himself and caught the younger.

"That's what testosterone can do for you."

The driver let Bones' comment pass. "Derek, help Bobby." Then he said to Maddock, "There'll be another time."

With the tip of his boot, Bones flicked the Steelers cap at the driver. "If you like going oh for two."

Maddock said, "You keep out of our way, and we'll keep out of yours."

The driver waited for his crew to walk past him, back toward the truck. "We'll see."

15

After driving past the farm once to see if anyone was there, they went straight to the Hilltop Barn. Maddock finished the conversation over his cell and parked behind the barn so that their vehicle wasn't visible from the road, and close enough to the back so that it'd be difficult to see from the house.

They'd traded their white SUV for a black one, and loaded it down with gear from the hardware store just before it closed. After spending the night, they'd left their luggage in a nearby town's hotel.

Bones told Maddock calling Tam would be a waste of time. Maddock wasn't going to admit his friend had been right.

Tamara Broderick was the leader of the Myrmidon Squad, a secret segment of the CIA tasked with investigating and countering dangerous groups, such as Trident. The exact goals of Trident were unclear, but they'd demonstrated keen interest in items of power associated with the ancient world as tools to further whatever those goals were.

Maddock said. "She had no information on why Trident might be here, and says to keep her abreast."

"So, you didn't mention the crystal Ruth gave us?"

Maddock opened the driver's side door. "You know Tam. More interested in telling people what to do than listening to what they have to say."

Bones grinned and opened the passenger-side door. "So, paying for our new ride and hotel stay never came up?"

The red-painted barn looked at least a century old, lending credence to the journal Bones carried. The barn's condition spoke to how well the Harshbinner family had maintained it over the decades. A pulley covered in surface rust hung from a bar above a swing-out door that opened into a loft. Maddock ignored the large sliding door, and the rope that dangled from the pulley down to it. He reached into his pocket for the key to the side door's new padlock.

Bones' gaze followed the line of poles bearing power lines to the isolated structure. The poles' weathered condition and the antique insulators concerned him. "Even money says the Mayans mined the copper for those power lines."

"No Wi-Fi then?" Maddock quipped.

The journal discussed wiring and lights installed to help the brothers excavate the mud and debris. It also mentioned explosives set to go off. No purpose or reason for the need to have such a contingency was given.

Maddock pointed to the gravel leading up to the cement ramp in front of the barn's sliding door. Delicate flowers with browning petals had sprouted up between the rocks. "No recent traffic in or out."

"The journal indicated electricity, but that doesn't mean it still works," Bones said, gazing back toward the house. "They might just store equipment in there, or junk."

"Or nothing," Maddock said, his hand brushing along the pocket holding the depleted crystal. "No sense debating."

The barn's interior was dusty, a nightmare for anyone with allergies. Splinters of morning sunlight shined through narrow gaps between some of the vertical boards.

A red Massey Ferguson tractor sat parked not far from the closed sliding door. Maddock was no expert, but its smaller size and exposed seat suggested it dated to the 1960s, maybe the 70s. In front of him rested something with wheels, bins or boxes, and something rotary beneath them. It was some sort of planter. A disk plow rested beyond the tractor.

Several built-in shelves stood against the walls using the twelve-inch beams as bracing hooks. Old hammers, tongs, bailing hooks, shovels, post-hole diggers and more rested on the shelves or hung from nails and hooks. Scattered crates and bins lined the walls. A coating of dust said the tractor, and everything else, hadn't been disturbed for several years.

Bones rested a hand on the tractor's seat. "Dude, farming with this must've sucked."

Maddock couldn't argue. A far cry from modern tractors with enclosed, air-conditioned cabs, and GPS to assist planting.

Wooden slats nailed to a pair of parallel beams formed a ladder up to the overhead loft. Maddock spotted a few bales of straw, or maybe hay, up there. The cement floor looked decades newer than the barn's stone foundation.

Bones strode over to the south wall. He pulled out his Maglite to supplement the scattered narrow shafts of sunlight.

Maddock watched Bones' beam follow the wiring. He reached over and pressed a push button switch. Two of four incandescent bulbs lit up. One attached to a rafter lit up the hayloft. The other highlighted several cans of oil and a grime-covered funnel lying on a tool bench.

Bones continued following the wiring under the loft. A twisted gaggle of wrapped electric wires ran along a beam and down into a galvanized pipe set into the cement floor. A wooden feed bin concealed the pipe from view, unless you went along the side to look for it.

Two framed boxes above the bin each held a knife switch. They looked beyond old-school, like props from a black and white Frankenstein movie, used when the mad doctor wanted to turn on the juice. Both, with the handle hanging down, were in the disconnected position. The wires leading to the top switch had been cut and wrapped in tape brittle with age. In addition, an antique padlock kept the switch from being lifted to the on position.

Bones looked closer. Slaymaker? Someone had probably tossed the antique lock's keys on some shelf two decades before he was born. He called over to Maddock, "The wires got to be the key. Looks like they go into the cement here."

Maddock agreed. According to the journal the brothers had strung lights in the cavern. And some demolition boxes. He moved over to his friend and appraised what Bones had found. "The wires could go down right there, paralleling an entrance to the cavern. Or, there could be an elbow in the piping, carrying the wires anywhere under the cement."

He tapped his boot on the floor. "This has been around a while, but I don't think it dates back to the nineteen forties or fifties."

"Metal detector?" Bones asked.

Maddock lifted the lid to the antique wooden feed bin. It had a divider, forming two compartments. Scraps of wood, cut boards and plywood from various projects over several decades filled both sides.

"We might have to move this to follow the pipes," Maddock said. "Looks sturdy, but could be heavy."

"Maybe heavy for a pair of white dudes." Bones grinned. "Luckily you have me."

Maddock laughed. "What we don't have is a metal detector." He looked over at a sledgehammer on a low shelf, leaning against the wall. "I don't think Mrs. Harshbinner would appreciate us breaking the floor on a hunch."

Sunlight entered the room as the side door opened. A snarling Doberman Pinscher stalked in, followed by a busty brunette wearing a stained cotton shirt, bib overalls, and carrying, of all things, a pitchfork. Sweat, mud on her boots, and bits of straw stuck in the frayed bun she'd put her hair up in suggested she might've actually been using the farm tool.

Bones appraised her. A little on the short side, well-muscled—in a feminine way—and wide brown eyes. A 9.25 for sure. Unless she smelled like manure.

"We don't take well to trespassing around here." Her voice held both conviction and confidence.

Maddock smiled and put his hands on his hips. The young woman was still near the door and the guard dog, still showing teeth and growling, remained at her side. "We've heard that one already. We're not trespassing. Mrs. Harshbinner invited us here."

"Right," she said, eyeing the two men with suspicion. "Dolph, sit."

"If you're from around here," Bones said, "you know that dude, Deputy Collins. Check with him. I'm Bones, short for Bonebrake. He's Dane Maddock; he's just short."

"Whatever," Maddock said.

Unfazed by Bones' attempted humor, she said, "Or, I could check with Ruth Harshbinner."

"You could do that," Maddock said, hoping she wouldn't take that route. One call, potentially informing Johnny or, worse, Trident, of their presence was bad enough. "She won't hear the phone ringing with her roommate blaring the TV and her hearing aids turned off." He shrugged dismissively. "Unless you've got all day, I wouldn't trust the Mallard Creeks' staff to get her to the phone quickly."

The woman leaned on her pitchfork, giving the two men a second appraisal.

"Or call Pari, Mrs. Harshbinner's grandniece," Bones suggested. This girl looked to be five or six years older than Pari, but it was worth a shot. "She's the one who connected her with us."

"Pari, huh?"

Maddock moved to pull his cell from his pocket. Dolph stood up, snarling. He held up his phone. "I have Pari's number, if she isn't working at the moment."

"Dolph, sit," the young woman said. She pulled her cell from her pocket. After a quick exchange with Deputy Collins she smiled and relaxed, petting Dolph on the head. The canine looked up at her, tongue lolling out to the side.

"Dolph?" Bones asked.

"I'm a Dolph Lungdren fan." Her expression went stony, her voice flat. "I must break you."

Both Bones and Maddock laughed.

"I'm Brenda," she said, flashing a Colgate smile.

"Bet she's a farmer's daughter," Bones mumbled.

"So, what are you doing in Mrs. Harshbinner's Hilltop Barn? Are you ghost hunters?"

Maddock saw she was serious. "No," he said, stepping around the planter and making his way to Brenda. Bones followed. "Mrs. Harshbinner asked us to do some videotaping for her."

Brenda squinted one eye at them. She tipped her pitchfork toward Maddock. "Are you looking for what her son's looking for?"

"I'm not sure," Maddock said. "From what the deputy said, Johnny hired a crew with a backhoe to dig up his mother's outhouse."

Brenda giggled, then put her hand in front of her mouth. Dolph continued to sit, panting, but keeping an eye on Maddock and Bones. "He's probably been reading from the wrong book."

Both Bones and Maddock maintained their poker faces. "Why would you think we're ghost hunters?"

She ignored his question. "Where are you two from?"

"South," Maddock said. "What about you? You must live nearby."

"Dairy farm across the field. Not the wanna-be industrial pig farm whose manure lagoon stinks to high heaven when the wind blows this direction." She frowned.

"Didn't hear any car or truck drive up," Bones said.

"Saw your SUV and rode my bike."

Bones quirked an eyebrow. "Tricky with that pitchfork?"

"You guys don't exactly answer questions, do you?" She put a hand on her hip. "You must be the guys who beat up Don Murphy's boys."

She observed them, then smiled. "You *did*. That makes you okay in my book." She flipped her pitchfork so that the tines rested on the cement. "They're asking around town, trying to find out about you two. Johnny is too."

"What are people saying?" Maddock asked.

"Not much. Johnny'll probably get his fancy lawyer on it. Hands out his attorney's business cards to folks he don't like." She grinned. "Bet you got one."

Maddock kept a straight face, but Bones smiled.

"Thought so."

Maddock nodded his head in approval. "You didn't answer why you wanted to know if we were ghost hunters."

"'Cause, this barn's haunted." Her eyes grew wide and serious. "Me and Pari's seen him. Mrs. Harshbinner has too. And so did her husband, Harold."

"Harold?" Maddock asked.

"Okay," she said, spreading another Colgate smile. "Just trying to catch you. Harvey Harshbinner. When I was younger, and finished with my chores, I'd come over and help Mr. Harshbinner.

"Anyway," she continued, "he told me about the ghost he'd seen, so one night when Nelli was sleeping over, we snuck out and into this barn. And wouldn't you know it. The ghost of Mrs. Harshbinner's uncle showed up, standing over by where you were, holding some sort of hourglass. At first I thought it was a lantern." Her eyes focused over by the feed bin. "Sort of blueish in color. We were too scared to run, or scream. He just looked at us for a minute, waved and then sort of faded down into the floor."

She looked at Maddock and Bones with a skeptical

eye. "You probably don't believe me."

"We've seen a lot of things people wouldn't believe," Maddock said.

"That isn't an answer."

"Let's just say our experiences make us more likely to believe your story."

"That still isn't an answer," she said. "But better than I get from most."

Brenda picked up the pitchfork, then shifted it to her left hand. She squinted one eye, then came to a decision. "Did Mrs. Harshbinner hire you two to videotape what's talked about in her father's diary?"

"Diary?" Maddock said.

Brenda rolled her brown eyes. "Let's quit beating around the bush, guys. I spent a lot of time with Mr. Harshbinner. Johnny hated getting greasy and smelling like gasoline. So I was like his son—more like a grandson 'cause Johnny's older than me. I helped Mr. Harshbinner repair mowers and did odd jobs. He helped me build a competition riding mower and took me to the pulling contests."

"Lawnmower pulls?" Bones asked.

"Sure." Brenda's face took on a wistful look. She sighed and scratched Dolph behind the ears. "Off and on, during all the time we spent working, he told me about the diary, and stories about what's hidden on this farm. He hinted it was hidden beneath the barn."

Maddock and Bones exchanged glances.

"It's what Johnny wants," she said. "Wants to contest the new will. It gives the property to the church instead of him. He's saying his mother isn't competent in her thoughts anymore." Brenda frowned. Her voice fell to just above a whisper. "Him and his lawyer might win.

Last couple of years, her mind's been slipping. Sometimes pretty bad."

Maddock and Bones exchanged glances again. So, maybe Ruth Harshbinner was going to lose the farm, and anything beneath it.

"Do you have a metal detector back on your farm?" Maddock asked.

Brenda cocked her head, thrown by the question.

"To follow the wires," Maddock explained. He gestured to the wall and the old switches. "There's supposed to be lighting below. Following those will give us an idea where." He tapped with his boot. "Under this."

Brenda shot Bones and Maddock a movie star smile. "I know exactly where the entrance to the cavern is. I'll show you, if you let me go down with you."

When Maddock and Bones didn't say anything, Brenda added, "I'll even do the videotaping for Mrs. Harshbinner, if you want."

Time was a factor, with the potential for Trident to get involved. Maddock scratched his head. Brenda would be a complication, if they let her videotape, especially if they found anything out of the ordinary. While Harvey Harshbinner had obviously shared with Brenda, Maddock didn't know how his wife would feel about it.

"Sure," Bones said, always the more impulsive of the two, and interested in having a good-looking woman around. "We're not exactly on a tight schedule, but this is a side-job favor."

Brenda flipped her pitchfork around so that the tines were pointed up again. "You know my family runs a dairy farm. What exactly do you guys do?"

"We're contractors for the government," Maddock

said, which was not completely untrue; they did occasionally work for Tam Broderick and her Myrmidon squad.

"You might look good in some of the video shots," Bones said.

"Very funny," she said, looking down at her work clothes. "Maybe if I clean up." She walked past Bones, winking up at him, then began tapping the wooden end of her pitchfork against the cement, listening. Then she took three paces away from the wall and tapped until the *thud* sounded less solid, more hollow.

"Figured it out myself one time, and Mr. Harshbinner smiled at my ingenuity." She continued tapping, forming an outline scraped in the dust with her boot. "Never exactly said if I was right but, when he wasn't around, I used my softball bat to check every inch of the cement floor." She finished her circuit, leaving a three by three-foot square just a little further from the wall than the feed bin. "This is it, or it ain't anywhere."

Dolph came to sit next to her, watching the two men with curiosity.

"You get the sledgehammer," Maddock said, nodding over to the low shelf were one leaned against the wall. "I'll go get the video camera."

It wasn't long before Bones had the area cleared out, tossing the broken pieces of cement and scraps of plywood from their position covering a metal door.

Maddock took a quick video shot with the camcorder of what his partner had uncovered. It was an older model, but still fit in his hand and, had three hours of memory and two backup batteries, one of which was now charged, leaving them two. He'd plugged in the third using one of the barn's outlets.

"You were right, Brenda," Maddock said while Bones put the sledgehammer back in its place. She grinned from ear to ear.

He knelt to brush away the last few bits of broken cement and examine the door. It was plain steel with rivets and painted black. A few of the rivets had a light patina of rust showing through. There was no handle or visible hinges. It appeared to be set into a metal frame built into the cement.

While it contained sketches and descriptions, the journal had nothing about the door, other than the keys. "Get me a piece of paper," Maddock said to Bones.

His friend tore a sheet containing advertisements from the back of one of the old manuals on a shelf.

Maddock took the paper and folded it once, then slipped it into the gap between the door and metal frame. "Four inches thick."

"Looks like what they make manhole covers out of," Brenda said.

Bones nodded. "It'll be heavy."

"Not too heavy for you?" Brenda teased.

"You didn't let me finish," he said. "Heavy for Maddock."

Maddock ran the paper along the crack. Twice, on opposite sides, it ran into something. "Some bar or mechanism is holding it in place." He crouched above the door, examining it. "Either we'll have to find the keys, or chip and break out this entire frame. Or get a cutting torch."

"Jackhammer would be faster," Bones said, "but louder. And you can't find them down at a Walmart, or the local hardware store."

Maddock leaned close again and ran his finger

across two divots in line with some of the rivets. He pulled out his pocket knife. After a moment he'd dug out bits of wax that had been poured in, on top of a cork. Using his Maglite, he said, "Looks like something screws in and there's two holes at the bottom, like something is meant to slide into them."

Bones leaned close and ran his fingers inside the hole Maddock had cleared out. His index finger barely fit. He felt the ridges, threaded for a bolt. The two holes at the bottom were maybe an eighth of an inch in diameter, with a shallow curving groove leading up to each. He pressed his finger in again, as far as it would go. "If the door's four inches thick, the holes are only about two and a half deep."

"Keys on the mantle." Maddock snapped his fingers. "Be right back."

Bones and Brenda exchanged glances as Maddock hurried out the barn's side door.

When he returned, Bones was petting Dolph and regaling Brenda with the highlights of their adventure in Hocking Hills with Connie and Nelli. Maddock held up the cast iron rings that had been screwed into the side of the mantle. Both he and Bones had mistaken them for nothing more than decorations.

He tossed one to Bones, who examined it. The ring was attached to a threaded post with two short prongs extending from the end.

Immediately he and Maddock began screwing the keys into place, using the iron ring as the lever. When they'd nearly screwed them completely in, they began hearing metallic scraping beneath the door, followed by a pair of clicks.

"Get the video camera running," Maddock said to

Brenda as he and Bones stood and then bent over and gripped one of the rings. On three they lifted the heavy metal door. Several grunts came from each man as they hefted it to the side and rested it on the cement floor.

Both Bones and Maddock trained their Maglites down into the hole, revealing a square opening about an inch and a half smaller on either side than the door. Round slots showed in the metal framing where round bars from the door had been retracted when the prongs were engaged and turned.

A metal ladder was affixed to a stone wall. At the bottom Maddock saw what he thought to be a landing, and then possibly a set of stairs, either poured concrete or carved into the stone. He guessed the former.

"Flip a coin to see who goes first?" Maddock asked Bones.

"Screw that," Bones said, climbing in. He descended the nine-foot ladder and then looked up, rubbing his hands on his jeans. "Ladder's got some serious rust going on."

"If it will hold your fat butt up, it should be sturdy enough for me," Maddock said.

Bones smirked, then pointed his Maglite. "See that pulley up there?"

A rusty pulley hung from one of the main beams.

"There's another one like that over there, and one outside," Brenda said, pointing at another high beam. "Mr. Harshbinner used it to get stuff up and down from the hayloft. The one outside hardly works, but the ones inside should."

"Probably how they lowered equipment in and lifted mud, rocks and debris out," Maddock said.

"Mr. Harshbinner said he'd been told the barn was

built to hide what's underneath it."

Maddock nodded at her comment, recalling that's what the journal said as he watched Bones descend. Then he went over to the door and began unscrewing the keys.

Brenda watched him, but didn't say anything. Unlikely as it might be to happen, he didn't want someone to arrive and lock them in. Nobody, except possibly Mrs. Harshbinner, knew where they were. And he didn't want to count on the memory of an old woman rehabbing in a nursing home. As he unscrewed the keys, the locking bars extended. When Maddock finished, he walked over and placed the keys on a shelf already filled with an array of wrenches, old drill bits, boxes of nails and more.

Bones had a little trouble taking the stairs. What had been carved out for standing room hadn't taken someone who was nearly six-foot-six into consideration. Nevertheless, he continued. He'd been in far more cramped and dangerous cave formations.

Maddock sat and slid his legs into the hole next. The Doberman Pinscher watched him from a few feet away, now easily eye to eye.

"Shouldn't I go next, to videotape?" Brenda asked.

"Let us check it out first," Maddock said. "There's supposed to be explosives placed down there."

"Why?" she asked, her brown eyes going wide.

Maddock shrugged. "To make sure nobody else could claim whatever they found?"

"Looks like mostly limestone," Bones said, his voice sounding muffled and distant. "Must've been a fracture in it, allowing the sinkhole that originally caught their interest."

Maddock made his way down the ladder and then the stairs. The air was damp and cool, probably a little over fifty degrees, what he expected. He made his way to stand next to Bones in an eight-foot wide area that ran left and right for about twenty feet. Rotting barrels, buckets, tins and old oil lamps were stacked on the stone floor and natural shelves created by erosion. Water dripped from the ceiling, forming scattered shallow puddles.

Both Maddock and Bones had studied a little about geology. Maddock figured that sometime in the past, parallel faults caused areas of the limestone to drop, forming a graben, or rift valley. And then, over the centuries, geologic movements and erosion had done its work. He spotted some stalactites, white, which meant they were probably formed from calcite. But they were relatively short, being only a few inches, and many appeared to have been broken, probably during the excavation, as the ceiling was only about six feet from the floor.

The cavern's floor looked to have been shoveled out, probably soil and rock debris that built up over the centuries, reaching past the most recent ice age. Maybe longer. He and Bones would be able to estimate based upon the length of the stalactites and height of the stalagmites. According to the journal there were some that were just over three feet in length.

Maddock wanted to go through some of the boxes and tins to see if there were any more crystals, but Brenda had made her way down.

"Wow," she said. "This is so cool!" Then she shivered as she videotaped. "Literally, it's cool."

"It's like a giant root cellar," Maddock said, "but

deeper, so it'll remain a constant fifty degrees, or a degree or two warmer."

"This place hasn't seen light in a few decades," Bones said. "And before the Mixon Brothers, it may never have been seen by man."

"So, that makes me like the sixth person to see it," the dairy farmer said. "Maddock being five and you, Bones, being number four. And Harvey number three." She frowned, memories of her friend and mentor stirring up.

After a moment Bones said to her, "Don't touch any of the crystals or other formations. They're fragile and oils from your skin will permanently damage them."

Maddock recalled several of the basic sketches, remembering that the cavern extended further northwest, toward the dairy farm and southeast, possibly extending beneath the road.

As if she were reading Maddock's thoughts, Brenda asked, "How big is this place?"

Bones answered, "Maybe up to a mile of tunnels."

"Cool as this is, I can't hang out that long." She frowned. "And dark. I mean, unlike city folks, I know what it's like without lights at night, but this..."

"That's okay," Maddock said. "Mrs. Harshbinner asked us to do it, and to give her our opinion on anything of value down here."

Bones began to wander off while Maddock continued talking to Brenda, hoping she'd leave so he and Bones could get busy.

"Government contractors?" she asked Maddock.

"We've done more than our fair share of cave exploring, here in the United States and across Europe and parts of Asia."

Brenda checked her watch, obviously not happy. She handed Maddock the camcorder. "Dad's gonna be wondering about me. Milking waits for no one."

16

Maddock and Bones followed her up the ladder and watched her leave. They then began unloading the SUV. They'd picked up extension cords, halogen lights, extra flashlights, bottled water, sacks and snacks, and more. While Bones moved the equipment into the entry room of the cavern, Maddock set up the motion detectors and security cameras, one of each outside the barn, focused on the doors, and one of each inside the barn, mounted in the loft, facing down. He then linked them into their cell phones and tablet computer. Maddock smiled, thinking it should be Corey Dean setting this up and watching their back for trouble. Luckily, Maddock had picked up a few of their friend's electronic tricks along the way. Corey wasn't around, which meant Maddock and Bones didn't have the luxury of hoping nobody from Trident, or even Johnny himself, showed up.

The last thing Maddock did was set up the cell phone booster to relay signals down into the cavern. Maddock placed the electronic gear they'd picked up from a shop near the hardware store so it wouldn't be immediately noticed. Anyone with keen interest or eyesight wouldn't be left in the dark for long. Hopefully they'd be more interested in the extension cords and other obvious signs. Intruders failing to realize they'd been detected would give him and Bones time to respond.

By the time Maddock checked the wireless connections to his cell phone and tablet, Bones had already finished hauling the equipment and setting it up within the cavern. The final preparations Maddock made were to hold the large sliding door in place with a two-by-four, and brace the side door closed with another two-by-four. He further blocked it with a heavy crate. On a last, possibly paranoid thought, he moved the cast-iron keys into one of the seed driller's grain boxes.

Once back down in the cavern, he asked Bones, "How are we doing?"

Bones set down the rolls of white and blue electrical tape. "I've been following the wiring, marking which wires go to the lights and which go to the steel crates."

Bones pointed to another knife switch, which was both locked and in the off position. "This one goes to the nearest box, filled with TNT, according to the journal. I didn't mess with it. TNT's more stable than dynamite, which the brothers thought about using—it would've become mostly nitroglycerin by now." He ran this tongue across his teeth. "Will the boxes still blow if an electric current is sent into the explosive booster?"

Maddock shrugged. "Those guys were probably amateurs."

Bones showed him the first box dug into one of the walls where there was a fracture in the stone. "There's a steel box encased in the wood. Moistures rotted the boards. The steel doesn't looked rusted through. Probably pretty thick."

"There's five of these," Maddock said of the box packed with TNT. It wasn't a question. More of verification, based upon the journal.

Bones nodded. "I've found two already. The last one is placed beyond where the lights' wiring runs." He pulled out the journal and flipped to a page near the back. "Near a deep fissure in the ground."

"Seems the brothers were more interested in readying to destroy the place than explore it," Maddock said.

"They did years of digging," Bones replied. "The lights they ran outdid any oil lamps for sure."

Maddock couldn't argue. He showed Bones how to access the cameras and motion detectors on his phone and the tablet, then asked, "Search together or separate?"

"A lot of area to cover. Should start with the boxes and old equipment first."

"If Ruth Harshbinner hadn't had one of the crystals," Maddock said, "I wouldn't give any chance of finding anything down here. Where Trident was harvesting them down in Mexico, it was a lot further underground. Dangerously hot conditions that required environmental suits."

Bones recalled the Cave of the Crystals. Tam Broderick lost one of her team there. "Could be someone just stashed some of those crystals here."

Maddock nodded in agreement. The Mixon brothers weren't the first to discover and explore the cavern they found under their farm. Maybe, in addition to some of the crystals, there was some hidden Atlantian or other advanced equipment the crystals powered.

"Split up?" Maddock asked. "If our cell phones lose signal, we can break out the two-way radios."

They'd picked up a pair of the inexpensive walkie-talkies. Limited range, but the gear Maddock had set up might not reach everywhere in the cavern complex.

"Na, Bro. Let's stick close. Search in tandem."

"Tandem, huh?" Maddock grinned. "Practicing fifty-cent words to impress Brenda?"

"Nope. Dime store words to addle your tiny white-dude brain."

Six hours later, after finishing a snack of beef jerky and water, Bones grimaced in frustration. The shadows across his face formed by the scattered incandescent bulbs that still worked, ironically, seemed to highlight his disappointment.

They'd checked most of the cleared southeast passages. They discovered hundreds of pristine calcite stalactites and stalagmites, some over three and a half feet in length, along with spectacular iron oxide and manganese dioxide formations. Six offshoots that hadn't been cleared, each identified within the journal, were dead ends with nothing of value. Mud and debris that the slow flow of time and water had packed in them over the centuries, remained there. What the brothers had accomplished while keeping their discovery a secret was monumental. Still, that meant potentially extensive unexcavated passages might lead to hidden chambers holding crystals, or even ancient technological artifacts.

Maddock measured and compared his results with stalactites identified and measured by the brothers over seventy years before. Through conservative calculations, estimating no more than a quarter of a millimeter's growth in that time span, any offshoot passage having calcite formations in excess of six-inch lengths were deemed at least 20,000 years old. That offered plenty of leeway, knowing their measurements and calculations weren't exactly scientific. Nevertheless, it narrowed the search by over fifty percent.

Maddock's knowledge, coupled with scholarly studies, placed Atlantis's destruction between four and twelve thousand years ago. So, passages with 20,000-year-old calcite formations would predate Atlantis and similar cultures. They'd be unlikely to contain what he and Bones were seeking.

Bones leaned against a damp wall, looking at the dirt and grime covering him from head to toe. "We should shower at the hotel and plug their drains instead of Mrs. Harshbinner's pipes, unless you think Johnny's going to inherit the place."

Maddock heard his friend and nodded as he turned the pages of the journal. "Why wouldn't they list where they found the expended crystal?"

"Why would they need to?" Bones replied. "Something they wouldn't forget."

Maddock re-examined the journal's cut-out portions and shook his head. Nothing directly or in context suggested the expended crystal Maddock carried in his pocket.

It'd take months of manual labor to clear everything out. If he and Bones didn't find anything in the next few days, Tam Broderick could send her people to finish the excavation—if Ruth Harshbinner retained possession of the farm, and allowed it.

Bones said, "What if Mrs. Harshbinner's husband got the crystal somewhere else. She might've forgotten and just made up what she didn't remember?"

Three hours later, they'd covered nearly a mile of passages. Some they had to crawl for yards to access, but most maintained a ceiling height between four and seven feet and ranged from two to six feet wide, with rooms that, while low in height were like expansive rock shelves that had dropped several feet. Those were littered with delicate calcite formations. The cramped, dark, damp and shadowy conditions didn't wear on the veteran explorers like it would most men and women. The tedium, however, did.

After examining every nook and cranny in about a quarter of the mapped area, and replacing their Maglite batteries for the third time, Maddock and Bones were about ready to call it a day when both of their phones vibrated.

They hurried a short way back to where they'd left the tablet. The grainy black and white video feed showed Brenda in jeans, boots and a plaid shirt. She stood outside the barn, knocking on the door. Dolph, her canine companion trotted over and sat down next to her.

"She's the type of woman that'll get loud if she has to wait too long," Bones said, making his way back down the narrow cavern passage. "Luckily, we're beyond Podunkville's suburbs, so only corn, beans, and cows will hear her."

With their luck, Maddock thought, *probably not.*

The fact that Maddock and Bones hadn't done any recording drew a suspicious look from Brenda. They allowed her to do some video recording while they lowered the extension cords and other equipment down into the cavern before locking it up for the evening. That appeared to placate her.

Bones had just dropped down the end of the last 150-foot extension cord to Maddock when he heard Brenda's startled scream.

Even though there were scattered lights where she'd

gone to video record, Maddock grabbed his heavy-duty Maglite and raced down the series of passages. By the time he reached Brenda, she'd stumbled some distance without a flashlight.

"Maddock!" she said. "I saw that ghost. I think I got a few seconds recorded before the damn camcorder died." She paused, a confused look on her face. "My flashlight died too, at the same time. Then the ghost disappeared. Sort of faded back into the dark."

Bones trotted up, hunched down to avoid the low ceiling. "What's the deal? Worms and centipedes shouldn't bother a farm girl like you."

She scowled at him. "If you saw a ghost, you big jerk, you'd be surprised too."

"I wouldn't scream like a girl," he teased.

"Whatever," she said. "I got it on camera. You'd've probably ran home to your mama."

Maddock laughed, but knew otherwise. Anything paranormal would've piqued his partner's curiosity. Even more, Bones would rather die of fright than try to live down squealing and running.

Bones led the way back through the cavern, past where Brenda said she saw the ghost. Nothing.

"Let's get up top," Maddock said, "and see what you recorded."

Brenda raised an eyebrow. "So you believe me when I say I saw a ghost?"

"We've seen a lot," Bones said. "Ghosts are supposed to drain batteries. Maybe that's why your flashlight and the camcorder died."

Maddock went up the narrow stairs, headed for the ladder first. Before Brenda followed, Bones asked her, "Did you feel a chill at the same time?"

"Well, yeah," she said. "I felt a quick chill, like standing in a walk-in freezer. That's what startled me into…well, screaming—a little." With a pursed-lip smile, she looked up at Bones who stood hunched over again because of the low ceiling. "That, and my flashlight leaving me in the dark—with a ghost."

Bones gestured for her to go up the stairs. "You wouldn't be the first chick creeped out by a ghost."

Maddock had retrieved the cast-iron keys before Brenda made it up. Fortunately, Dolph just sat and watched him.

They slid a fresh battery in the camcorder and packed around the tiny preview screen.

"Right about now," Brenda said, anticipation in her voice.

No ghost. But two seconds before the recording ended, glowing light, about waist height, appeared. It was reminiscent of foxfire's bioluminescence except, instead of pale green, it was a steely cobalt blue.

"That's weird," Brenda said, rerunning the end sequence. "Maybe ghosts are like vampires. You can't see them in mirrors or film them." She looked up at Bones and Maddock over her shoulder. "You guys haven't seen any vampires ever, have you?"

"That would be a negative," Bones said. "Ask me about aliens, and you won't get a straight answer."

Unsure how to take that response, Brenda asked, "You guys ever watch that alien-astronaut dude on TV? The one with the hair that stands up straight, like he's seen a ghost?"

Bones made a face. "Whoa, chick! That dude rules!"

"Seriously?"

"You know how Muslims don't want people

disrespecting their prophet?" Maddock said. "That's how Bones is with the ancient aliens guy."

Brenda rolled her eyes. "You guys are strange."

17

After a steak dinner at a bar that doubled as a restaurant, Maddock and Bones made their way back to the hotel, both men remaining aware and on their toes.

He'd given his cell number to Brenda, in case she saw anything going on at the farm. The motion detector and camera mounted outside the barn were still set up, but a live set of eyes, even if at a distance, couldn't hurt.

However, at the moment, her eyes weren't of concern.

He didn't have to say anything. Bones knew it too. Someone was watching, if not following them. There were too many people going in and out of the ice cream parlor and coffee shop, and the teenagers out walking and cruising in their trucks, to narrow any suspects down before they reached the hotel.

They passed by the old brick hotel and made their way to the end of the street to cross at the light. Maddock put in two quarters to get a local paper from a machine in front of a closed barber shop while Bones pretended to answer a call on his cell.

Bones caught sight of one of the young men they had the run in with, one of Don Murphy's sons. The young man was standing with one foot on a bench, smoking a cigarette and talking to a heavy-set girl wearing a scruffy T-shirt and patched jeans. Bones made eye contact and the young man quickly looked away.

"It's one of those boys we ran into," he told Maddock. "Bobby."

Maddock tucked the newspaper under his arm. "No reason farmers can't visit more than one town in the area."

Bones nodded agreement. "Shouldn't be a problem. I'll move the rental to another lot."

"Good idea," Maddock said, like Bones, figuring ways to head-off pointless trouble. "I'll get us a different room, under another name."

At 3:32 am, Maddock stirred awake. A shadow's movement outside the window did it. Bones was already sitting. A sliver of light from a nearby street light made its way between the drawn curtains that led to the balcony. That, and the alarm clock's glow, made Bones visible in the otherwise inky darkness.

Bones held a finger to his lips, encouraging Maddock's silence.

An unnecessary gesture in Maddock's estimation. That meant something had Bones spooked.

Two sets of footsteps sounded in the hallway. Maddock also heard the scrape of metal on metal and a muffled word or two from outside, to the left of their balcony.

In unison the two men slipped on their pants and boots, and their holstered pistols. Maddock, his Walther, and Bones, his Glock. Maddock silently moved toward the balcony's sliding door while Bones crept to their room's entry door.

A cell phone's *ding* broke the silence. Someone had just received a text. The sound of breaking glass followed.

When Bones heard the door to the room he and

Maddock formerly occupied open, he opened his door and slid out into the hallway. At the same time Maddock stepped out onto the cement balcony just in time to see a man enter their former room. The balcony along the rear of the hotel overlooked the parking lot and small park beyond. A three-foot railing made of wrought-iron enclosed each of the balconies.

Maddock stepped over the railing and leaped the eight feet toward the next-door balcony. As soon as his foot found purchase he stepped over the railing and crouched low, before looking into the dark room.

Someone holding a flashlight gave muffled orders. "Check the bathroom. Pull that door closed."

Maddock recognized the voice. Bobby the farmhand, one of Don Murphy's sons.

Someone responded to Bobby's order to get the door, but not fast enough. Bones dropped the intruder with an open-palm strike to the face, breaking the man's nose. Before Bobby could train his flashlight on Bones, Maddock rushed in and knocked it from Bobby's hand, and wrapped him in a choke hold.

Someone between the beds stood momentarily confused and earned a kick to the stomach. Bones didn't bother to stop and admire his handiwork. Instead he surprised the final intruder exiting the bathroom. A punch to the face sent him stumbling back into the bathtub, lapsing into unconsciousness.

Bobby struggled to loosen Maddock's grip to no avail. He still smelled of stale sweat and cigarettes. Maddock whispered into the farmhand's ear, "Care to explain what you're up to?" Maddock loosened his choke hold so the young man could speak.

"Just doin' what we're told."

The dark figure of Bones loomed up in front of Maddock and his captive.

"Which is?"

"Scare a couple of outsiders. Get them to leave—hey, you're them!"

It wasn't difficult for Bones and Maddock to guess who sent them.

"Nope. We're your worst nightmare," Bones said. "Nighty night." A quick jab to the jaw knocked Bobby out.

Bones shut the door leading to the hallway and turned on the light while Maddock stepped over the broken glass and closed the balcony door's curtains.

"This guy's the assistant night clerk," Bones said, pointing to the first man he'd taken down. He was skinny and in his mid-twenties. "One that gave us our first room. Must not have known we switched."

"Going to take some serious dry cleaning to get the blood out of that white shirt," Maddock said. Blood from the clerk's nose was all over his shirt and staining the beige carpet. He picked up Bobby's cell phone. It had a passcode.

Maddock tossed it to Bones.

Bones examined it and frowned. After wiping with a bed sheet to remove their fingerprints, he dropped it on the floor. "Hope he took the insurance option." A quick stomp shattered the glass screen and internal components.

"Best to just leave them here." Bones said. "Let them try to explain."

Maddock nodded in agreement just before his cell phone began to vibrate. He pulled it from his pocket. "Brenda just texted. Someone's over by the farmhouse.

She's going to check it out."

Maddock texted her back. *Don't go over there. We're on our way to check it out.*

He waited for a second, then sent, *Respond.*

After a few seconds, both he and Bones went back to their room. While Bones finished dressing, Maddock tried calling Brenda. It went straight to voicemail. He didn't bother leaving a message.

"Hurry up, Maddock," Bones said, grabbing their packed duffel bags. "I'll drive."

18

From a distance, Maddock and Bones saw several windows in Ruth Harshbinner's farmhouse lit by internal lights. Bones raced up the driveway, toward a late model Dodge Ram. Its diesel engine was running, and its driver's side door was open. The headlights shined on an older man crouched on the ground. He was talking into his cell phone while stroking a trembling Doberman Pinscher. Maddock thought he recognized it as the same dog that had been with Brenda earlier.

Bones skidded to a stop, allowing Maddock to jump out a half second before him.

"I don't know where she is," the man nearly shouted into his cell phone. "Her flashlight's on the front lawn, and they took a shot at our dog." The man stood and turned to see who was approaching him. "Just get here as quick as you can."

Maddock slowed, holding his hands in plain sight. "Are you Brenda's father?"

"I am," he said, his gaze shifting from Maddock to Bones. "Who exactly are you?"

"Mrs. Harshbinner hired us to do some work around her house," Maddock said.

"You're that Indian fella that beat up Don Murphy's boys. Brenda told me you two were working out here."

Maddock asked, "What happened?"

"Why are you here?" Brenda's father slowly approached. He was on the lean side, wearing stained coveralls and a John Deere baseball cap. His eyes squinted in suspicion. At his side, Dolph gazed dully up at them. "What made you show up just now?"

Maddock said, "Brenda texted me about twenty minutes ago that she thought she saw someone around Mrs. Harshbinner's house. I texted back, telling her to stay where she was. When she didn't answer, I tried to call and got voicemail."

"That doesn't say why you're here."

"Ruth Harshbinner's son, Johnny, was caught trespassing, and his mother changed the locks. We thought he might've been trying to break in, and we told Mrs. Harshbinner we'd watch out for that."

"Well, if it was Johnny, he shot Dolph, and Brenda either ran off or he took her."

Maddock's breath caught in his throat. That explained why the man was treating them with such suspicion.

"Grazed Dolph's leg." The man looked down at his dog, seemingly trying not to think about the possibility that Brenda had been abducted. He gestured to the hind leg with a bandana tied around it. "Just a graze, thankfully." He swiped his thumb across his cell phone's screen. "Sheriff's on the way. I better call the vet."

When the man began talking into his cell, Bones whispered to Maddock, "Let's go. We'll get tied up with the sheriff if we stay."

"We're going to go see if we can find Brenda," Maddock said.

"What?" the man asked. "You know where she is—where Johnny took her?"

Maddock and Bones backed toward their SUV. "We don't know if it was Johnny," Bones said. "We're just going to cruise the roads and hope we get lucky."

They climbed into their vehicle and Bones sped down the driveway. They were a quarter mile away when they passed a crossroad. Down it they saw the flashing red and blue lights of a deputy's car.

"Where to?" Bones asked.

"Well," Maddock said, "if it's Trident that took Brenda, they probably don't have much familiarity with the town. Only place they would know—"

Bones finished the sentence with his partner, "—is Johnny's print shop."

"You remember where his shop is?"

Bones nodded and stepped further down on the gas pedal.

Johnathan Harshbinner's print shop stood just off of Main Street. It took up half of the first story of a brick building that was well over a century old. Above it were two stories of old apartments. The streetlights showed the apartment windows to be dirty with no curtains and several having pigeon droppings scattered around. That suggested they were unoccupied.

The print shop had a large display window to either side of the street entrance. A gray Lincoln Town Car from the late 70s sat with its engine running across the street. It was in near pristine condition, and that probably said something, but Maddock wasn't sure what. The driver sat smoking a cigarette and observing the minimal street traffic. Lights were on somewhere in the back of the print shop, but nobody was in the front area that Bones or Maddock could spot as they drove past. Lights didn't necessarily mean anything as the antique shop next door, as well as several other businesses on the street, maintained internal lighting, probably to deter burglars. But those businesses that did have lights on, had them in the display windows or front areas.

"Park around the corner so we can go around back," Maddock said. "If there aren't stairs to the apartments, there might be old fire escapes."

Maddock was right. A rusting metal framework of fire escapes lined the back of the building. The alleyway running between the backs of the buildings was relatively clean. It held a few old tires and some broken pallets and several green dumpsters. Maddock had definitely seen worse.

Avoiding line of sight from the print shop's back door window, they climbed atop a dumpster to jump and reach the fire escape's bottom platform. Using his knife in the dry-rotted wood, Bones had little trouble prying one of the old apartment's back windows open.

Their flashlights revealed that Johnny used the apartment above his shop for storage. Boxes of paper, old folding and cutting machines and dusty file cabinets filled several of the rooms. The trick was trying to make their way across the room without causing the floorboards to squeak.

Maddock discovered a door, apparently barred or padlocked from the outside. The lock was meant to keep people out, not in. With little effort, he removed the pins from the hinges. Then Bones easily pulled the door back from its frame, bending the cheap hasp in the process.

The stairs led down to a narrow hallway. One door opened onto the street. One on the left wall probably went to the antique store. The one on the right, to Johnny's print shop.

The old door had a modern deadbolt, but also

narrow frosted windows built into it. Both men listened, and heard muffled voices. They sounded deep, deeper than Brenda's, but that didn't mean she wasn't in the print shop.

Bones took his knife and began prying at the wood holding the glass in place. "Not very security conscious," he whispered back over his shoulder.

Maddock replied, "Small town."

Two minutes later Bones handed the antique pane of glass to his partner and reached in, turning the dead bolt's latch to unlock it. Definitely not security conscious.

They stepped into the dark work area. Light from an office, ahead and to the right cast long shadows as it played over various types of equipment: offset printers, cutting and folding machines, a silk screening machine and dryer and a table filled with folded stacks of t-shirts. To the left, leaning next to the doorway that led to the front of the shop, with its counter and display area, stood a burly man in a dark suit. White shirt and no tie, like he'd left a wedding reception. A bulge under the jacket suggested a handgun.

The man smoked a cigarette while observing passing traffic through the shop's front windows.

To the right, where fluorescent light emerged from an open door and window with Venetian blinds only partially closed, sounds of conversation emerged.

"Those two guys," a distressed feminine voice said. It was Brenda's. She spoke with a bit of a lisp. Maddock recognized it as someone speaking with a swollen, probably tender lip. "I don't know their names. They just told me they were hired by Mrs. Harshbinner to do some video recording and watch the house."

"Watch for what?" asked a deep voice. The man sounded like he gargled gravel in his spare time.

"They didn't tell me."

A *thud*, preceded a brief scrape of metal on tile. It was joined by a sudden gasp of expelled air, followed by a groan.

Only half glancing back, white teeth revealed the man watching the shop's front was grinning.

Wordlessly, Bones nodded his head toward the grinner. The pair split up, with Maddock moving behind the cutter, toward the table laden with shirts.

"Well, do you want to rethink that last answer?"

Maddock figured they hadn't been here long. Brenda looked like a tough farm girl. She probably had loyalty toward Ruth Harshbinner, but probably not so much for he and Bones. And she certainly hadn't had training to resist harsh interrogation. If these were Trident men, they were just getting started.

Maddock used Brenda's voice to mask the little noise he made approaching the back office.

"They didn't say," Brenda said, quickly adding, "but I can guess…if you want me to."

"Let me hear your supposition," the gravelly-voiced man said. "And then I'll decide." He paused. "If your supposition lacks insight, Arnie will break several of your ribs. Then we'll return to your attractive face. Arnie loves to break teeth."

Several heartbeats passed before the dairy farmer started talking, hesitancy in her voice. While she spoke, Maddock crouched low and peered a half second into the office through the open door.

"Mmm—Mrs. Harshbinner doesn't want her son—Johnny—on the property. He's got a lawyer from out of town and wants to take her farm."

Maddock spotted three men in the large office. A tall man with frizzy gray hair and narrow mustache stood between Brenda and the doorway, blocking most of Maddock's view of the woman. She was blindfolded and duct taped to an office chair. Behind her was a desk filled with papers, a tower computer, several flat screen monitors and a landline phone. Beyond the desk, along the back wall, were shelves filled with papers, manuals and several bowling trophies. A heavyset man with thick sideburns leaned close to Brenda, wearing close-fitting leather gloves. Arnie. He was doing the punching.

Blood covered Brenda's chin as it seeped down from her swollen lower lip. Another man, in his thirties, Latin American from his hair and skin tone, leaned against one of the shelves in back, observing.

All were dressed like the man watching the street, in black suits with white dress shirts. And all carried firearms in shoulder rigs under their jackets.

"Where did Ruth Harshbinner get the money to hire the two men—what were their names?" the frizzy, gray-haired man asked. Maddock guessed his rough voice was due to years of smoking.

"She still owns the farm," Brenda said, "so she's got money—and I told you, I don't know their names."

The Latin American man nodded and checked his cell phone. "Chloroform her."

Arnie, the heavyset man that had been punching Brenda, reached into a pocket.

"What?" Brenda asked. "No."

Arnie opened a dark bottle and poured some clear liquid onto a handkerchief.

Maddock knew it was his chance. His Walther

already drawn, he knew Bones was waiting for him to make his move. At least two of the three men would be focused on Brenda, maybe all three, while they were putting her under. That was his best chance for surprise.

As soon as the handkerchief went to her nose, Maddock stood in the doorway, pistol aimed at the Latin American man—the apparent leader, and shouted. "Hands up, and freeze."

Without hesitation, the Latin American man dropped his cell and went for his pistol. The gray-haired man went for his gun too, albeit a fraction of a second slower. Arnie grabbed Brenda and spun the chair between him and Maddock in the doorway. He dropped the bottle and went for his gun while keeping the chloroform-soaked handkerchief clamped over Brenda's nose.

Maddock fired. The Latin American man staggered back into the shelves with a bullet buried in his chest just to the left of his sternum. The gray-haired man had his gun drawn before taking a bullet to the belly. He staggered back, dropping his pistol and collapsed to his knees, clutching his stomach. By the time Maddock shifted his aim to the last man in the office, the heavyset opponent had hunkered down behind Brenda, with his gun drawn.

"Now what're ya going to do?" Arnie taunted. "Drop it or—"

With no safe shot to take at Arnie as he had the others, Maddock adjusted his aim and pulled the trigger. His bullet slammed into the squatting man's knee as it protruded from behind the cover of Brenda and the chair.

The big man hobbled and toppled onto his side, but

didn't give up his gun. Before the Trident operative could take aim at Brenda, or Maddock himself, Maddock pulled the trigger again, taking the Trident man in the forehead.

Maddock rushed into the room and kicked the pistol away from the kneeling gray-haired man. He looked up at Maddock while sagging to a prone position on the floor, blood seeping from between the fingers of both his hands. "Call an ambulance," the man gasped.

"I aim to do that in a moment," Maddock said, looking over his shoulder, back into the print shop's work area. The guard was on the floor and Bones was taking on the man from the Lincoln. From somewhere the Trident man had gotten a ball peen hammer. He, however, wasn't trained in hand-to-hand combat. Bones ducked under his roundhouse swing and took the man in the ribs with his knife. A quick head-butt by Bones ended the fight.

Their eyes met and Maddock hurried to check Brenda. She was still blindfolded and taped to the chair, and she was unconscious, but breathing steadily. He examined the brown glass bottle on the floor. The acrid odor of its spilled contents confirmed what the label read: Chloroform. She'd be out for a short while, but okay.

The old man on the floor was already going into shock. Maddock had witnessed more than his fair share of mortal wounds. The expanding pool of blood suggested that no matter what Maddock did or how fast the EMTs arrived, the gray-haired man would be joining his two dead cohorts.

"Your guys?" Maddock asked.

"Out for the count. Both should survive," Bones said.

"Brenda?"

"Knocked out. Chloroform," Maddock said, striding over to the desk. "Get their cell phones." Taking a clean shop rag from the nearby shelf, he lifted the desk phone and dialed 911.

While there might be ballistic evidence, nothing else would tie Maddock and Bones to the scene. Brenda had been blindfolded and unconscious. Neither of Bones' foes had gotten a good look at him in the dark work area. What would be obvious was that Brenda had been kidnapped, likely by these folks. And if the bullet that struck Dolph could be recovered, that would link one of these men to the abduction scene. Who took the kidnappers down would hopefully remain a mystery.

The 911 dispatcher's voice calmly asked, "911. What is the nature of your emergency?" The landline provided an automatic location.

Even if the gunshots hadn't been heard and reported, law enforcement would be dispatched to the print shop to investigate the call.

Maddock checked on Brenda again, and then, without a word they headed out the back way, using the shop rag to remove any fingerprints on the side and upper door along the way.

19

Rather than parking their SUV at the farm, leaving it visible either from the road or Brenda's family dairy farm, Bones and Maddock hiked the short distance from a sheltered pull-off. Deep grass and weeds said it wasn't used often. Plus, the trees and brambles would keep the rented vehicle out of sight. They didn't have anything to carry as everything they needed was in the cavern beneath the Hilltop Barn.

They waited, out of sight, while the deputy sheriff drove off. Brenda's father followed in his Dodge Ram. Brenda had been found. In any case, there wasn't much evidence outside the farmhouse to gather. Yellow tape strung along the porch marked the house as part of the crime scene. The county's sheriff's department would likely call in help to collect any potential forensic evidence.

Nothing had been disturbed within the barn, and the security cameras were still working, so Maddock and Bones locked and braced the doors closed before using the wrought-iron keys to lift the door to the cavern. Maddock picked up the video camera that had been plugged in to recharge and downloaded the video to the tablet before uploading the file to his Dropbox. From there, when he got the time, he could burn a copy to DVD and send it to Mrs. Harshbinner. That obligation out of the way, Maddock patted the pocket holding the discharged crystal given to him by the old farmer's wife, and joined Bones in finishing up their search for crystals.

He'd already texted Tamara Broderick, with an update so there was nothing else to do but search.

Bones had gone left so Maddock went right. He heard his friend complain, "You forgot to pick up some bulbs."

That was the plan, to pick up those and a few other items in the morning, before their return to the cavern. But, with the failed assault on them at the hotel and Brenda's abduction, and the likelihood that Johnny and his lawyer would already have been contacted about the dead bodies and Brenda being found in his print shop, the clock was ticking.

How long would it take Trident to respond? If they had more than an inkling that there could be hidden technology beneath the farm, they would've been all over it in force long ago. Like every organization, governmental, private and even illegal, Trident had limited resources and manpower. As their size and scope of operations wasn't yet known, the corresponding lack of ability to predict a response worried Maddock.

They had plenty of batteries, bottled water and food—Granola bars and frosted, blueberry Pop Tarts, the latter thanks to Bones.

Maddock examined a deep but narrow crevice. His flashlight's beam sparkled as it reflected off the water droplets and calcite stalagmites. No hint of any concealed shelving or compartments in the limestone walls and ceiling. He used a shovel to remove sediment, only to discover the same. Another dead end. A repeat of more efforts than he cared to count from the day before. He suppressed a sigh, backed out and moved to the next formation with potential, hoping his partner was having more luck.

Rather than pick up where he left off, Bones decided to start at the back and work toward the entrance. He made his way, following the strung lights, every fourth or fifth one working. The rusted metal domes over each bulb limited their reach, but also kept the water that dripped occasionally down from shorting them out. That the wiring and some of the bulbs still worked said a lot. Old-school manufacture. They didn't make them like that anymore.

That said, he had little more success than Maddock for the first few hours. Then, down one of the wider branches, Bones caught a faint hint of blue light. It wasn't yellowish from an incandescent bulb or the whiter variety from his flashlight. It reminded him of the cobalt color of eyeshadow his last date had worn, except hers didn't glow.

The light faded. It didn't flicker out or just shut off, but faded like a dimmer switch had been dialed down.

Bones shined his flashlight up at the ceiling. His Maglite's beam was getting weak. He tapped his flashlight and returned to examining the ceiling. Wiring for the lights didn't extend down that hallway, but other wiring did. He knew what that meant. One of the brothers' boxes filled with explosives. They'd checked before starting the first day, and those wires remained disconnected. Beyond that, the knife switches were locked in the off position. Still, decades-old explosives were certain to be unstable.

Thinking about that, he switched out the batteries in his flashlight and set the weak ones down on a rock shelf. He'd grab them on the way out.

Just as he was about to proceed, the blue light appeared again, then faded. Like before, it disappeared like someone had used a dimming switch.

Ducking low to avoid his forehead hitting the twelve inch long, carrot-shaped stalactites, Bones followed the muddy branch as it doglegged to the right. He had to turn sideways, his jeans scraping the limestone as he worked his way through.

The light ahead of him returned, this time more intense, strong as a forty watt bulb, which was a lot in the darkness, other than his Maglite's narrow beam—which began fading. Bad batteries?

He completed the turn and stopped. He stood up straight in surprise, and bumped his head on the angled limestone above. Not far in front of Bones stood a man clad in a gray, loose shirt and dark trousers, and holding a lantern. The pale man's short hair was messy and his face and hands were covered in swaths of mud. His skin—his whole body—was backlit by gray light. Bones squinted. It wasn't gray backlighting. The light emanated from the man, who lacked all color except for the cobalt blue washed along his right-hand side. The intense blue glow emanated from the lantern.

The figure stood still, slightly hunched, not because it had to. Bones sensed it was the weight of years. He'd seen this man before…a picture on the wall above the fireplace mantle. This was one of the brothers, the lost uncle. *A ghost.*

Perhaps he should have found the sight bizarre, wondered if he were losing his mind, but he and Maddock had some limited experience with contacting the beyond; enough to not reject what he was seeing.

Bones and the ghost of the brother starred at one another for a moment. Bones decided the man was holding a metallic framed hourglass, not a lantern. His heart raced, seeing the same ghost Brenda had. He, however, wasn't going to run away, screaming. He was standing face to face with a real ghost.

"Dude, you're Ruth Harshbinner's uncle," Bones said, reaching into his jacket's inner pocket. He pulled out the journal. "You're Hue Mixon, Vernon's older brother."

The ghost leaned closer, seeming to focus on the journal.

The beam of Bones' flashlight faded a little more. He turned it off and pulled out his cell phone. After bringing up the screen he tapped on the camera icon. As he did, Bones watched the battery level on his phone cascade downward, from eighty percent down to sixty. A wave of cold washed over him. By the time the camera feature loaded, the cell phone battery power read thirty-five percent. With his thumb, Bones clicked a photo of the ghost, still staring at him, tipping his head a little to the left, then back to the right.

His phone went dead. The weak light from the bulbs behind him were mostly blocked. The phosphorescent glow from the ghost lit no more than itself, but the blue hourglass, it seemed to radiate enough to reflect off the damp limestone.

"Hue," Bones said. "Hue Mixon, Ruth Harshbinner—that's her married name. You knew her as Ruth Mixon, Vernon's daughter. She gave me and my partner this journal. We came down here to locate the rare crystals, like the one hidden in the pages of the journal." Bones paused, trying to assess the ghost's response.

The gray image of Hue Mixon stood up straight.

"Maddock," Bones called over his shoulder. "Get

over here."

Then he returned his focus on the ghost. "Hue, can you show me where the rare crystals are?"

Hue's ghost raised the hourglass and flipped it over. Then he backed away, turned and faded as he continued down the cavern's passage.

Bones started to follow, but everything was dark as black ink. He couldn't see his hand in front of his face. He pulled out his flashlight and clicked it on. The beam shone at one-third its normal strength. That was good enough.

It wasn't a difficult choice. There was only one direction to go and impossible to get lost. Bones called one more time for Maddock over his shoulder, telling him, "I'm down the passage where I left a set of batteries." Hunched low, Bones followed the ghost. If Maddock wasn't listening, or able to hear, it'd result in his missed opportunity.

20

Maddock's cell phone chimed and vibrated in his pocket. Activity around the outside camera had triggered the notification. Maddock activated the icon with his thumb, drawing in the halting black and white feed, all the while trotting back toward the entrance.

A white van with Lake Star Movers painted on the side and a 1970s era Cadillac were parked outside the barn. Six men in black clothing, two with assault rifles, were approaching the barn.

Maddock made it to the tablet and tapped the screen, bringing it out of sleep mode. The screen showed the same scene as his cell, but in more detail. He quickly texted Bones: *Trident outside.*

Were some of the men wearing body armor? One of them pointed up at the camera. Seconds later the signal ended.

Up the rusted ladder he raced, hearing heavy banging on the barn doors.

Bones followed the passage for about thirty yards, around another dogleg turn. Several steps later the area opened up—both left and right, across and down. Leaning over the dark crevasse, his Maglite's beam didn't reach the bottom. The chamber ran about thirty feet to his right before pinching to an end, along with its walls. The same to the left, except only twenty feet. It spanned only ten feet across, but in most places there was less than a six-inch ledge, and eighteen inches at the most. Several white crystal stalactites at least three feet long hung down from the ceiling. Beneath one of them, near the far wall, was an equally tall, although a little more stout stalagmite. To the right of it was a rippled formation of iron oxide climbing the wall. To the left, the same orange color, but it appeared much of the delicate formation had been broken. In addition, the top of the stalagmite, instead of being white, held a muddy sheen, some of it buried beneath a recent layer of calcite growth.

It was possible that iron oxide had contaminated the water dripping from the ceiling and down onto the stalactite above, and caused the discoloration. Then again, Bones recalled that dirt and even oils from a person's hand could do the same to such formations.

He shined his flashlight's weak beam along the far wall. Something seemed odd about the area to the stalagmite's left, besides the disturbed iron oxide formation. The limestone appeared smoother than most other places within the cavern complex.

Bones didn't recall anything like this recorded in the journal.

He bent over to pick up a small rock in the mud at his feet. It was there he noticed the electrical wire going down into the crevasse. He leaned over and followed it with his flashlight, seeing it terminated into a box, the type the brothers had packed with explosives. And the box was tucked into a fissure about ten feet below him. Closer examination showed the fissure ran both under his feet and was present beneath the side opposite where he stood. It didn't take an engineer to figure that such an explosion could collapse this entire area, maybe half the cavern. That was if the decades-old explosives could still be detonated.

Maddock hadn't shown up. Probably didn't hear Bones call out to him. Trying with his cell phone was out. The battery was truly dead. He did, however, have the batteries he'd changed out sitting on a ledge where the passage branched off of the main one. The ones currently in his flashlight had no more than another fifteen minutes. The other set had at least ninety minutes. He could go all the way back for new ones, and let Maddock know of his discovery.

Bones shook his head. The ghost of Hue appeared for a reason. Wanted him to follow. Assessing the walls, and his experience as a free climber, it would be hardly a challenge to get to the other side. The brothers had clearly felt this area was important, and the ghost of Hue emphasized that. Maybe he wasn't heard from again because he fell down into the crevasse?

Backtracking to get the half-spent batteries just in case, and calling for Maddock one more time as a compromise, Bones decided the discolored stalagmite was the key. If he reached it, things would start happening.

Outnumbered at least six to one until Bones reached him, Maddock weighed his options. With only two magazines for his Walther, against two apparent M4 Carbines with thirty-round magazines, and certainly converted from semi-automatic, and probably everyone else armed with at least a pistol, the odds were long against him. Not only were these guys better armed, they were certain to be better trained than those he and Bones had dealt with at Johnny's print shop.

Climbing up into the loft would offer him surprise, but after that, limited his possibilities. If he stayed on the ground level and could work his way around and out the door, he might lead them away. He checked his phone. No reply from Bones. He could dial 911, but that would draw the deputy sheriff responding into a situation where he—or they—would almost certainly be outgunned.

He checked his cell phone again. There was no way he could go back after Bones. They'd both be trapped in the cavern.

A few moments later someone began prying the sliding door open with a crowbar. The brace was holding the side door closed, but the boards were coming apart under someone's boot or shoulder. How they knew to go to the barn? Maybe they got some information from Brenda before Maddock and Bones arrived at Johnny's print shop. Or, someone had pumped information from Ruth Harshbinner in the nursing home. Whatever the case, they weren't there to talk.

Maddock turned off the lights, including those in the cavern before sliding along the wall, behind the equipment, making his way to the old planter with its bins. If he could draw their attention, he and Bones might get them in a crossfire.

Bones climbed out to his left, and made his way along the damp and occasionally slick limestone wall. At several spots, his shoulders bunched as his fingers clamped on like vices while he sought out elusive toe holds.

By dropping a stone and listening, Bones had

estimated the drop into the crevasse was at least two hundred feet. The splash confirmed what his flashlight suggested, that the bottom was filled with water. How deep was anyone's guess.

"That would make for an ugly fall," he muttered, inching back from the edge.

Cutting back where the cavern walls pinched together was the trickiest part, but his training and physical condition reduced the effort to a minor challenge. Soon he had the ledge, the protruding twelve inches, making the final stretch feel like walk in the park.

When Bones reached the stained stalagmite, he removed the Maglite from between his teeth and examined it. Something about it suggested a lever rather than a simple mineral formation. Gripping the top he attempted to move it like shifting gears in an automobile. Pressing right to left caused the crystal formation to shift.

Several clicks beneath it followed. Then a scraping rumble in front of him, beneath his feet. A slab of the limestone, six feet high and three feet wide, swung back, away from Bones, opening like a door.

21

The sliding door gave way first. Two men entered, keeping low and moving the barrels of their assault rifles from left to right, searching for a target.

From outside a nasal voice said, "Dane Maddock and Uriah Bonebrake, we know you're in there. Lay down any weapons you may have and vacate the area."

Right, Maddock thought. *Like that's going to happen.* His limited encounters with Trident operatives didn't lend credibility to the suggestion that he and Bones would be allowed to leave uninjured and without question. He wanted to check his cell phone to see what was up with Bones, but any light from the screen would give his position in the shadowy barn away.

Maddock's question as to whether he should shoot first and ask questions later was answered a handful of seconds later, when one of the assault rifle-armed men shouted, "I see one!"

Even as Maddock shifted to a better angle behind one of the planter's tires, the order from outside came.

"He had his chance to surrender. Take him out."

A three round burst ricocheted off the planter's steel frame.

Maddock popped up and fired off two shots, the second taking the shooting man in the shoulder. In the barn's shadowy darkness, limited to slivers of light coming between some of the boards and the half-opened sliding door, Maddock noticed the shot man was stocky and bearded. The hitman grunted and fell back.

Two more men wearing black jackets and knit caps, and holding pistols, entered the barn.

Maddock moved back to get behind the disk plow. It wasn't the best position, with the barn wall lined with shelves and a few boxes and crates behind him, but he couldn't stay in one place too long.

"He was over by that trailer with the boxes," the shot man said, apparently not down.

He was wearing body armor, Maddock thought. He preferred his Trident opposition wearing white shirts and black sport jackets.

"I think he moved," the shot man continued.

One of the pistol-toting men said, "George, hold your position. Greg and Diego. Fan out and close. Burt, you watch for anyone in that hayloft."

Someone outside, near the door asked, "Hayloft?"

"Up there," the man replied, keeping low but pointing up with his pistol.

"Got it, Boss." The reply had to be Burt's.

Four men were inside the barn, and that left two outside, counting Burt. Movement of those two just beyond the door told Maddock, if he made it there, and despite Burt not being too bright, he wasn't home free.

While the men were rearranging their approach, Maddock took advantage of the momentary confusion. Using stealth learned in SEAL training and improved upon over the years, Maddock slid back to his position behind the planter. He reached into one of its bins and pulled out one of the cast-iron keys.

Bones pressed on the stone door. With less than a few pounds of pressure, it swung wide open into an octagonal room. It had a flat ceiling supported by eight pillars set several feet in from the eight corners. Overall the room was no more than forty feet across.

Lying on the floor before them were the skeletal remains of two warriors. Their weapons and armor identified them as Egyptian. Most likely these men had been selected, or perhaps had even volunteered, to guard this place for all eternity.

A blue glow emanated from somewhere within the room, from behind one of the black marble pillars. The same color he'd seen with Hue's ghost. Bones' flashlight caught something reflective on the room's far side but, before stepping in, he checked the door. Inside the frame were two pairs of holes about three inches in diameter set across from each other. One was near the top and the other near the bottom. Bones examined the door. It was about ten inches thick with corresponding holes set into it. They were aligned so that something could slide into the shafts, locking the heavy door in place.

Warily he stepped back and pried loose a slab of stone near his left foot. It was thick and heavy, and perfect to wedge in the door so that it couldn't swing closed.

That accomplished, he trained his flashlight's beam into the room once again.

To the right of the door sat a black marble, waist-high pedestal. Its top was empty, with a roughly six-inch diameter, quarter-inch deep depression carved into it.

Directly across the room was a rectangular crystal the size of a coffin. It rested on a base made from black marble, identical to the pillars. The floor was inlaid with hexagonal stone tiles about an inch across. Its design depicted a night sky filled with stars. Bones recognized the central star formation to be that of the constellation Orion. The walls and ceiling were made from some sort of stone, not a porous type. Within it were swirling gray and black lines.

"Whoa," Bones said, and breathed in the stale, dry air before stepping into the room. The lack of moisture was at odds with the cavern behind him. "Out of this world." Forgetting it was dead, he reached into his pocket and pulled out his cell phone to record what he saw.

Shrugging at the phone's failure, Bones continued forward, his eyes switching back and forth between the blue glow emanating from behind the far pillar on his left and the large crystal block directly ahead.

Upon reaching the pillar, Bones stopped. Sitting with its back against the black stone pillar was a desiccated body wearing the brittle remains of boots, black trousers and a gray shirt. Bones knelt and added his Maglite's beam to the glowing blue light. It didn't require the metallic blue hourglass resting on the dead man's lap to recognize him. Hue Mixon, the older of the two brothers. The ghost he'd seen less than ten minutes before. That Brenda and her friend had seen in their youth. That Ruth Harshbinner's husband had seen, causing him to never visit the Hilltop Barn at night ever again.

Then his eyes turned back to the crystal block. From kneeling level there appeared to be something held within it. He stood and shined his flashlight down into the crystal. Although frosted on the sides, leaving it semi-opaque, looking down from above it was clear, like lead crystal.

Inside was a female body, not decayed like Hue's, but

with eyes closed as if she were simply asleep. She was tall and thin, her arms and legs a bit too long. Metallic blue rings adorned her long fingers and rubies encrusted the buttons lining her white gown. No sign of any of the power crystals he and Maddock sought.

What stood out the most, however, was the woman's head, the shape of her skull.

Bones bobbed his head and altered the angle of his flashlight, finally moving around to his left, to the head of the crystal coffin. He couldn't immediately tell if the crystal simply encased her like a perfectly sealed coffin, or if the crystal fully engulfed the body, like an ancient insect entombed in amber. He guessed the latter, or she was resting on a clear crystal surface.

The apparent shape of her head wasn't due to a distortion caused by the crystal, or the way her dark hair had been gathered and pulled tight along the back of her scalp. Her skull was elongated with a bulging mass the size of a tapering cantaloupe that protruded along the parietal and occipital bones.

"Dude," Bones said to himself, "Maddock's got to see this. It'll bring back memories."

Sensing something amiss, Bones turned to his right. Standing at arm's length behind him was Hue's ghost. In his left hand he held a blue glowing hourglass. Bones looked down to see that the blue metallic device was no longer in the mummified corpse's lap. The ghost held *the* hourglass.

"Hue," Bones said, staring down at the gray apparition with elements of blue light penetrating into his incorporeal form. It seemed to infuse the ghost with ripples of energy.

The ghost reached out and touched Bones' flashlight.

Immediately the light beam's intensity increased. In doing so, the ghost's luminosity temporarily faded. Then he reached out and touched Bones' cell phone that he'd never pocketed. It too came to life, and the ghost faded a little more.

Bones' cell phone vibrated in his hand while its ringtone—"Rock Bottom" by Kiss—told him he'd received a text from Maddock.

"Figures," Bones said. Hesitant to look away from Hue, anticipating that, like in so many tales and movies, the ghost would disappear when he did, he glanced down at his cell phone's screen. *Trident outside.*

Bones immediately pocketed his phone and turned toward the exit. That text could've just been sent, or sent ten or fifteen minutes ago. How the cell signal made it down this passage didn't matter.

Hue's ghost interposed himself between Bones and the exit and held out the hourglass for Bones to take. The strain on Hue's face and the way the blue time device wavered and lowered, showed the ghost was struggling to maintain his grip on the hourglass.

Bones didn't have time to ask or wonder. "Thanks," he said and snatched it as if out of midair. "There's some folks in the barn that need their asses haunted." The warm blue metal sent what felt like a weak current into his hand, feeling like when he was a kid and touched a nearly depleted nine-volt battery to his tongue. Ignoring the sensation, he raced toward the doorway, picking up speed, hopefully enough that he could clear the ten-foot crevasse.

22

Maddock knew waiting was a losing proposition. They'd find and box him in and take him down in a crossfire. They had more guns and greater firepower. He needed to go on the offensive.

He took the cast-iron key and tossed it so that it hit the floor and skidded near the back corner, behind the disk plow. He then popped up and fired two shots into the assault weapon-armed man he'd shot before. This time he took him in the hip and left hand. He then spun and sent a shot at one of the pistol-armed men. He ducked back down, not waiting to see the result of his third shot. Good thing. A spray of bullets snapped by over his head, while others slammed into or ricocheted off the planter's metal framework.

Crawling along the wide length of the planter, Maddock heard thumping and scraping high up on the wall near the doors. Not taking the time to ponder its origin or meaning, he popped up again. Two men had fired at him while one had moved. The two shooters quickly shifted their aim. Since he had to rush, he took the easy shot. His bullet hit Burt, standing motionless in the doorway, distracted while looking up at something outside. The man's focus returned as he staggered back, right hand going to his wounded right bicep.

"Now, Bones!" Maddock bluffed. "Doorman's down."

Bones cleared the crevasse with two feet to spare. He had to slow to squeeze through the narrow dogleg turns until he reached the main corridor. Maddock or someone had turned off the lights. With only his flashlight, he couldn't run full out, having to watch for low-hanging rocks or stalactites, and debris on the floor.

The muffled sound of gunfire urged him on as he reached the entrance. Maddock was in the barn, along with whoever he was exchanging fire. After grabbing a burlap sack and flicking off his flashlight, he shoved the glowing artifact into the sack and slung it by the drawstrings over his shoulder. He reached out, grabbed hold of the ladder and began to ascend. Only faint light showed above, telling him the lights in the barn were out as well.

Maddock moved to the back of the barn, behind the disk plow. The Trident operatives were being much more careful in their movements. He was running out of options. A new round of gunfire hammered the disk plow and holed the barn's wooden wall behind him. He returned fire, hitting the second assault weapon-armed man, knocking him down. Maddock grimaced, knowing his bullet had little chance of penetrating the man's body armor. Instinct urged Maddock to dive to the side, and he followed its guidance. An eighty-pound bale of hay hit the spot where he'd just been crouching. The distraction, however, allowed the Trident operatives to close on him. With the muzzles of two pistols pointed at him from close range, the jig was up. Maddock dropped his Walther and stood with his hands held out in the open.

Four fresh men, two armed with pistols and two with pump shotguns, also dressed in black, rushed into the barn.

Maddock released a long breath. *Where the hell was Bones?*

23

Bones finished climbing the ladder as the gunfire abated. Glock in hand, he emerged and spotted four men in black garb racing through the half-opened sliding door into the dark barn. Three shots later, two were down. He dove for cover behind the nearby grain bin. Bullets and buckshot slammed into it and the wall beyond.

After the five second barrage, silence reigned. Maddock hadn't joined Bones—he would've recognized the sound of his partner's Walther.

"Mr. Bonebrake." The deep, calm voice came from the far side of the barn, back by the disk plow. Bones bristled at its nasal tone. "I have your partner, Dane Maddock, sitting, facing the wall, with my pistol pointed at his blond head. And my associate, Diego, has his assault rifle aimed at his torso in general, should I for some reason, miss."

The barn's overhead lights turned on.

"You have to the count of three to toss out any weapons before surrendering."

"Don't do—"

Maddock's protest was cut short by a *thud* followed by a grunt. Bones guessed a pistol butt to his friend's head. That, more than anything made him see red. He released a breath and forced his mind into a rational thought process.

He didn't know how many men were in the barn. At least four, one with a shotgun and one with some sort of automatic weapon. They had Maddock. If they wanted him dead, they would've shot him already.

Bones took another deep breath and released it. "Who exactly is asking for my weapon?"

"The infamous Uriah Bonebrake doesn't know?" The man's voice dripped with smugness.

Bones gritted his teeth. He hated his first name. "If I knew, asshat, I wouldn't be asking."

"Let us just say, the organization I represent has run afoul of you and your friend in the past."

Bones listened for footsteps, to determine if anyone was moving toward him. The only thing he heard was a few men on the ground, moaning in pain. And a mumbling voice or two, trying to reassure those injured.

"Afoul?" Bones asked. "I'm not asking about your breath, dude." As soon as he said it, Bones shifted to the other end of the grain bin.

Apparently finished with Bones' distraction, the man began counting. "One...two..."

"Okay, dude," Bones said and stood. He set his Glock on the grain bin and stepped away, and began counting men. Nobody shot at him. That was good.

Including the man he spotted up in the loft, there were ten. Four down, with one man tending wounds. Two near Maddock along the wall behind the disk plow, one behind the tractor and one near the planter, and the one in the loft. All were dressed in black jackets, pants, boots and knit caps.

"You all belong to some sort of beatnik cult?"

"Are you truly disarmed?" The man asking was the one near Maddock. How his friend sat was hard to tell from the distance and with the plow mostly in the way. Probably cross-legged, facing the wall. What was obvious, even from a distance, was the blood on Maddock's scalp.

"I was only carrying my Glock."

"No other weapons, Uriah?"

"Oh," Bones said, signaling with a raised hand. "I thought you meant guns. I have a knife too." He drew it and placed it next to his pistol.

"And in your shoulder bag?"

"A light," Bones said. He slowly reached over his shoulder and spread the bag open with his fingers, allowing some of the blue light to radiate out. "The off switch's broke." He pulled on the strings, closing the bag.

"A nightlight," the thin, nasally-voiced man said, holstering his pistol.

Bones shrugged. "Whatever, dude. What do you want?"

"Me?" The man pointed to himself. "I don't want anything. In a moment, I shall call my direct supervisor to see what *he* wants. The man turned away from Bones and spoke to the man holding the M4 Carbine on Maddock. "If he moves, shoot him." Then he looked back at Bones, offering a disingenuous smile. "What, may I ask, are you doing here?"

Bones figured they probably had an idea about the cavern, and they'd seen him come up out of the floor. Even a chimp like Nasal Dickhead could put two and two together.

"We were hired by Ruth Harshbinner to do some videotaping." He gestured toward the hole in the floor. "I could give you a tour of what we documented."

Bones didn't really think they'd let him down there. But, they might split up, giving him and Maddock a better chance to escape their situation. Even though he hadn't been able to remove the stone keeping the door to the hidden room open, odds of anyone finding that branch right away were slim. Just play along, feign cooperation, and wait for an opportunity.

With his head both swimming and throbbing, Maddock listened to the conversation between Bones and the Trident group leader. They'd frisked Maddock for weapons, but failed to check his pockets with enough care to discover the discharged crystal.

"Boss," someone called across the barn. "There's a hole in the floor, with a ladder."

"Well?" the leader asked.

Two pairs of boots clomped toward Maddock, while the distant man continued. "It's dark down there."

"I've got a Maglite in my pocket," Bones said. "If your flunky needs it."

One of the boot pairs belonged to Bones. Maddock kept a straight face. If his friend was volunteering his Maglite, he must have a plan.

"How generous of you, Mr. Bonebrake," the leader said. "What about—"

Bones cut him off. "There's old school light switches down there. Old school, like the ones on the wall. About half the bulbs work."

"My, you are cooperative" the leader said. "Attempting to earn brownie points?"

"I *am* kinda hungry. What about you, Maddock?"

The pairs of boots came to a stop about ten yards away.

"I prefer Twinkies," Maddock said. He started to turn his head and earned a carbine muzzle to the back of his neck for the effort, followed by a warning.

"Face the wall like the boss said or get a hole in your

head."

"You're a poet?" Maddock asked.

"Shut up," the carbine-wielding man said. "You shot my friend."

Keep him talking, Maddock thought. Of course Bones liked to talk and yank people's chains even without purpose. Maddock's head was beginning to clear. The throbbing? Not so much. "Who shot at who first?"

"Shut up."

At the same time, Bones shouted over his shoulder. "It's got fresh batteries."

"You gentlemen appear in jovial spirits," the leader said. "You realize there will be a price for shooting my men."

"Dude, like my man, Maddock, said, you all shot at us first."

"Come now, Mr. Bonebrake." The leader gestured by swinging the barrel of his pistol between himself and Bones. "The organizations of which we are a part have objectives."

"We're not a part of any organization," Maddock said.

The leader said, boredom reflected in his voice, "A part of, affiliated with, linked to…" He sighed. "Mr. Bonebrake, put the bag with your night light next to the wall. Once you do that, Rory will escort you gentlemen over to that corner." He glanced up at the loft. "Vernon, if they attempt to leave the corner or do something that makes you suspicious, empty your shotgun into them."

Maddock climbed to his feet, and placed a hand against the wall in front of him, hoping to disguise that he was still a little disoriented from the blow. He might have a concussion, but that was the least of his worries.

Bones reluctantly unshouldered the sack and set it against the wall, and followed the gestures Rory made with his M4 Carbine.

When they were over in the corner, Vernon revealed a buck-toothed smile, and trained his pump-action shotgun down on the pair. Rory backed off and split his attention between Bones and Maddock, and one of the injured men. They'd plugged the shoulder wound and stopped the bleeding. One of the men Bones had shot, they'd simply dragged over to the wall.

"Two of them are down in the tunnel." Bones looked at Maddock and frowned. "You okay? Much more blood and your blond hair is going to go ginger."

Maddock looked up at his friend. "A four Tylenol headache."

They watched as one of the men pried at the antique lock holding one of the knife switches in place, the one connected to the TNT-filled boxes. It didn't even seem to register to the moron prying with a screwdriver, that the wires leading to it had been cut and taped over. One of the other men noticed and began picking at the brittle tape covering their ends.

Maddock watched silently as another of the Trident operatives found a pair of bolt cutters and took them over to his not-so-bright Trident cohort. Probably Burt's twin brother.

Both his and Bones' pistols were sitting on the planter.

The leader had moved over by the grain bin. He peered down into the hole. "Anything?"

A muffled voice came up. "It's a big cave down here. There's shovels and halogen lights and a video camera. I looked at a minute and all they did was walk around and focus in on the fancy white rocks pointing down from the ceiling."

"Told ya, dude," Bones said. "The old widow just wants to keep her farm out of her greedy son's hands."

The leader's head snapped their direction. "Save your lies and misdirection for another time."

"See, Maddock?" Bones said. "There's gonna be another time. By the way, you *do* know, the new Twinkies aren't as good as the originals."

Maddock ignored Bones' comment and asked, "What's that?"

Out of the hole climbed a glowing apparition. Its form was semi-transparent, made up of varying shades of gray. The dim overhead lights and sunlight radiating in from the open sliding door washed out most of those.

"That's Hue Mixon, the brother that disappeared," Bones whispered, answering his friend. "We met briefly—tell you later."

The leader staggered back, pulling his pistol. "What the hell?" His nasally voice had gone up an octave and a half. "Who—what is that?"

The ghost ignored the leader, and everyone turning his direction, even the wounded on the ground lifting their heads to see what frightened their leader. Hue's ghost walked the several steps to reach the power switches. The two Trident operatives dropped their screwdriver and bolt cutters and staggered back, both paler than the ghost before them.

The overhead lights began to dim as Hue's ghost reached for the upper switch.

"Holy crap," Bones said. "Think those dolts connected the wires in the cavern?"

"What are you doing?" the leader asked, having recovered from his initial shock.

The ghost gripped the upper knife switch and lifted it into the on position. Sparks flickered and his vaporous essence faded. As he disappeared, rumbling blasts sounded. Through their boots, Bones and Maddock felt several minor shockwaves carried upward by the stone.

It didn't end there. Instead, the rumbling and floor vibrations intensified.

"Holy crap," Bones said again.

"Earthquake," Maddock replied, working to keep his balance.

The floor shook and cracked. The barn walls swayed. Tools hanging on the walls clattered to the floor. Vernon yelled as he lost his balance and, like the tools, fell to the floor. Staggering to keep his footing, Rory turned to see what had happened.

Bones and Maddock ducked low and shot forward. Bones was faster than his friend and plowed into Rory, driving the carbine-wielding man into the disk plow. He slammed his fist into the back of the Trident operative's head, driving his face into the farm implement's metal frame.

Bones pushed the unconscious man to the side. "Maddock, get the sack," he said, ignoring the dropped M4. Instead he raced toward their guns on the drill planter.

One gunshot rang out. Bones didn't know if someone shot at him or Maddock, or it was due to random panic.

Grinding pops preceded another major shockwave, this one dwarfing any previous. Bones and Maddock struggled to keep their feet.

"Let's get out of here," Maddock suggested.

Bones shoved their pistols into his belt. "How?" A Trident operative stumbled to his knees in the doorway, but otherwise kept his balance. He had a shotgun and was trying to aim it their general direction.

A jagged crack formed in the cement. It began near the hole and spread across the floor towards the opposite wall. The half of the barn Maddock and Bones were on rose several feet while the other side dropped. Then the earth rocked like an EKG showing a heart attack. Everything began to collapse into a chasm created from the cracked and crumbling floor. The old tractor dropped into the earth's widening maw, followed by the planter.

"Through the wall," Maddock said, tucking the sack into his arm like a football and hoping all the bowing and twisting had loosened the centuries-old nails; or, better yet, had sheared some of them holding the boards in place.

Feeling like he was Wile E. Coyote, Bones followed his partner's lead. Together they crashed shoulders first into the wall just beyond the disk plow.

The boards at the bottom gave way and the two men tumbled out onto the hard ground. Both men scrambled to their feet and raced downhill, away from the barn. All around them fissures and sinkholes were forming. Maddock immediately recognized the pattern. They appeared to match the layout of the cavern below.

"This way," Maddock shouted, and led Bones toward the farmhouse.

From the hilltop, down past the road, trees and swaths of turf tumbled into a jagged, spreading latticework of ravines. Behind them the barn collapsed, its ruin dropping from sight. Edges of the elevated fissure folded in and fell, smashing down and covering the roof and what remained of the barn.

Before they reached the house, the rumbling stopped. Still trying to comprehend their luck, Maddock and Bones sat down in the lane, the surrounding soybean plants ceasing their spasmodic dance.

"You'll never guess what I found down there," Bones said.

"A major fault line in the bedrock?" Maddock asked.

"You guessed it, bro. And those two brothers had packed it with a good load of explosives."

Maddock shook his head but stopped because of the pain. He rubbed the back of his head, feeling the crust of blood forming on the big knot. "Boxes of TNT," he said, "even strategically placed shouldn't have caused all of that—unless it was already poised to go."

"That's not the half of it," Bones continued, and told Maddock about the chamber and the body in crystal, and that ghost had drained his cell phone before he could get a picture—and then recharged it, so he received Maddock's text.

He saved for last, the contents of the sack sitting between him and his partner.

They both grinned, staring at their glowing prize—still unsure exactly what it was.

"We'll need to tell Tam and the Myrmidons about this find." Maddock paused. "Eventually, I mean."

Bones nodded, then crinkled his nose. "What's that smell?" It was like someone had dumped a dozen port-o-pots next to them. Both men stood up and surveyed the area.

"The earthquake redirected the stream near the

road," Maddock said. "And also, apparently, released the contents of the industrial pig farm's manure lagoon into it."

Both men knew whatever was down there in the cavern formation had been destroyed and buried beyond reach. The cesspool of manure pouring in served as a nasty icing on that cake.

Bones laughed. "Think Johnny will still want the farm?"

"Let's get to the SUV before anyone shows up with questions," Maddock said. "Sometime down the road, when things settle down, I'll send Pari the digital video files I uploaded."

"Like that's a priority," Bones said, lifting the sack holding the glowing metallic hourglass. "After we figure out what this is, it'll be Tam Broderick's turn to owe *us* big time."

The End

About the Authors

David Wood is the author of the Dane Maddock Adventures and several other series and novels. He also writes fantasy under his David Debord pen name. When not writing, he hosts the Wood on Words podcast. David and his family live in Santa Fe, New Mexico. Visit him online at www.davidwoodweb.com

Terry W. Ervin II is an English teacher who enjoys writing fantasy and science fiction. His current series include the *Crax War Chronicles* (SF), *First Civilization's Legacy* (Fantasy) and *Monsters, Maces and Magic* (LitRPG/Fantasy).

In addition to **Cavern**, a *Dane Maddock Universe* novel co-authored with David Wood, Terry has written standalone works, including a short story collection.

To contact Terry or to learn more about his writing endeavors, visit his website at www.ervin-author.com.